Love's Journey™
ON MANITOULIN ISLAND

Moriah's
LIGHTHOUSE

Love's Journey™
ON MANITOULIN ISLAND

Moriah's LIGHTHOUSE

BY SERENA B. MILLER

LJ EMORY
PUBLISHING

LJ EMORY PUBLISHING

Cover & Interior design by Jacob Miller.

Original front cover photo by Annette Shaff - Used by permission.

Author photos by Angie Griffith and KMK Photography
KMKphotography.com - Used by permission.

Published by L. J. Emory Publishing

First L. J. Emory Publishing trade paperback edition August 2017

For information about special discounts for bulk purchases, please contact L. J. Emory Publishing, sales@ljemorypublishing.com

Printed in the United States of America

10 9 8 7 6 5 4 3 2 1

ISBN 978-1-940283-27-2

ISBN 978-1-940283-28-9 (ebook)

To Steven

There is no fear in love, but perfect love casts out fear.

-1 John 4:18a ESV

Chapter One

Moriah Robertson lay motionless in the dirt beneath the cabin floor as she stared with sick fascination at the Massasauga rattlesnake loosely coiled upon a rusty water pipe only eight inches from her nose. The snake's delicate tongue flickered, tasting the air between them. Its head bobbed, getting a fix on the heat emanating from her breath. A dry rattle warned that it was not amused by her presence.

She held her breath, shut her eyes, and willed herself to lie perfectly still. She had known of people who had survived a rattler's bite, but all things considered—she would prefer to pass.

The ticking of her watch sounded as loud as a jackhammer to her adrenaline-sensitized ears. She continued to lay deathly still in the small crawl space beneath the cabin while she counted the seconds, mentally cursing the snake, the snake's mother and, while she was at it, the slow water leak that had forced her to crawl beneath Cabin One. A few feet away, Lake Huron lapped gently at the shoreline.

It was a gorgeous day for those not being held captive beneath a cabin by a stupid snake. It was sunny and warm. In fact, it was unusually warm for this early in the year, which was probably part of the problem. Snakes didn't move around in cold weather, which was one of the reasons she rather enjoyed winter. The other reason was that she didn't have to deal with guests when there was snow on the ground.

She heard a heavy truck crunch up the gravel driveway. It stopped at the resort's lodge.

"Moriah!" her Aunt Katherine, shouted, "It's a delivery for you. I think it's that part you've been waiting for."

Apparently, the new part she had ordered for the emergency generator had finally arrived. At least that was one less thing she could cross off her to-do list—if she ever got out from under this blasted cabin.

She did not know if reptiles had ears but, just in case, she chose not to respond to her aunt's call.

"Moriah?"

Moriah stayed mute.

She heard Katherine chat briefly with the delivery man and then the heavy truck shifted into gear and drove back over the driveway and out to the main road. Moriah winced as the screen door on the main lodge slammed shut.

She was suddenly, violently, envious of her aunt who would happily spend the day laundering the resort's sheets, blankets and pillowcases inside their nice, snakeless, lodge. As usual at this time of year, she and Katherine were preparing for the guests who would begin arriving in a few days. The fishing camp they owned was their main source of income.

There was much work to do before the guests arrived. She and Katherine had divided the chores between the two of them over the years. Her aunt tended to the indoor chores, and she took care of the outside ones. At least she normally took care of the outside jobs—when she wasn't immobilized by the presence of this stupid, stupid snake!

Heat radiated through the plywood floor directly above her face. The fire she had built in the cabin's wood stove early this morning to make sure the flue worked, was probably what had drawn the rattler out of its den. She could think of no other reason a Massasauga would be above ground in Canada this early in the spring, even if it was warmer than usual.

She counted to one hundred and cracked an eyelid. The snake had apparently chosen to ignore her. It crawled along the water pipe, its black underbelly rasping slightly as it slid over the rusting metal, inches above her quivering skin. She drew a shallow breath and held it.

When it had slithered well past her face, she exhaled. Slowly. Then an unhappy thought struck. Didn't rattlesnakes travel in pairs? She slid her eyes over to her right. Nothing happening there except an empty spider web and a drift of autumn leaves against the stone foundation.

Then she looked to her left.

The few remaining nerves in her body that had not been on red alert clanged an alarm. At least five other Massasaugas lay entangled several feet from her shoulder.

She closed her eyes again and fought panic. A victim could survive one rattlesnake bite, two maybe with medical help, but no one could withstand a multiple attack. Especially not while wedged into a location where a quick exit was impossible.

Just as she thought it couldn't get any worse, a heavy reptilian body slid over her right leg, and then her left. It demanded her last shred of self-discipline not to scream and start beating her fists against the bottom of the cabin floor. A spasm twitched in the calf of her right leg. A drop of sweat began a slow, itchy descent into the hairline above her left ear. She desperately wanted to scratch the itch, but that was not an option.

Then another unhappy thought struck. What if she were lying on top of the hole from which they'd emerged?

Sweat oozed from her body, soaking her flannel shirt. Her calf muscle did a jig beneath her jeans.

She checked again. The snakes shifted as the one that had crawled across her legs joined the pile.

What on earth was she going to do? She couldn't stay here forever. While she struggled to lay perfectly still, a long-forgotten memory floated into her mind.

When she was a child, she had seen a man at a circus seated in a screened box filled with diamondback rattlesnakes. They had buzzed and warned while they crawled all over him without biting. She had stood, mesmerized, until Katherine pulled her away.

There was one more thing she remembered about that encounter besides the memory of it giving her goose bumps. The man in the box had survived by moving extremely slowly.

Okay then. Since the snakes did not appear to be in a hurry to go elsewhere, that could be a plan. She might survive if she moved very, very slow. She dug her fingernails and heels into the dirt and began to inch her way out, butt-crawling in infinitesimal degrees toward the sunlight, expecting to feel the sting of fangs at any moment.

About an hour elapsed while she finessed her body the few feet necessary to be free of the cabin. At least she thought it was an hour. It could have been a week. Or a month. Time had lost all meaning while she was under there. The late afternoon sunlight struck her face as she emerged, unscathed, from beneath.

She was safe, but every muscle in her body was trembling, and her scalp felt like it was crawling with invisible snakes.

Once she was certain she had cleared the cabin, she leaped to her feet and practically flew over the pathway toward the lodge, putting as much distance between herself and the snakes as possible. Although she knew it wasn't possible that the snakes would be pursuing her, she still glanced back over her shoulder to make absolutely certain.

At that moment, she rammed into a stranger who had apparently been standing directly in her path. He felt as solid and unmoving as a boulder while she practically climbed his body and danced on his head. "What in blazes…?" he asked.

She clung to this marvelous human mammal, grasped both of his ears, gazed into his blue, wonderfully non-reptilian eyes and, emphasizing each word with a tug because she felt it extremely important he understand, enunciated carefully.

"I. Hate. Snakes!"

The stranger blinked, pulled her hands away from his ears, held her at arm's length and, in the type of soothing voice one might use with a wild animal or a lunatic, said, "Okay."

The stranger had red hair and freckles. She had a prejudice against men with red hair and freckles. A nine-year-old carrot top had made third grade miserable for her. Under the circumstances, however, she decided she might like to crawl inside this man's body and hide.

"There was a nest of them." She let go of him, stepped away, and wrapped her arms around her waist, giving an involuntary shiver.

"Where?" he asked.

Moriah pointed back toward Cabin One.

"You were beneath that cabin?" he asked.

She nodded vigorously. "I was trying to fix a water pipe."

Then she started shivering so violently that her teeth began to chatter. "There were snakes *everywhere!*"

"Oh, lass." His voice held the hint of Scottish burr. "No wonder you're as pale as a ghost."

At that moment the trees exchanged places with the lake and the lake moved over to where the line of cabins should be. She heard a roaring in her ears and then the ground rushed up to smack her in the face. *This is going to hurt*, was her last conscious thought.

But it didn't hurt because strong arms caught her just as everything turned black.

Chapter Two

Ben McCain saw the girl's green eyes roll back in her head, but he was so stunned by this raven-haired beauty running smack into him, that he barely recovered in time to catch her before she hit the ground. For a moment he simply held her beneath her arms while she dangled from his hands like a rag doll.

She wasn't all that small. In fact, when she had grabbed his ears and stared intently into his eyes, they had been nearly nose-to-nose. He was six feet tall and she was only about an inch shorter. One hundred and fifty pounds, he estimated, hefting her. It was an educated guess, based on a lifetime of working as a stonemason. He could evaluate the weight of a rock within a couple of ounces.

This girl surprised him. She looked a lot lighter than she felt. All muscle, he figured. Evidently from hard work. Her hands against his skin had been rough from callouses.

The physical strength he had built over the years came in handy as he squatted to get a better grip on her. Then he rose, cradling her against his chest. It would make sense to throw her over his shoulder in a fireman's hold, he supposed. It would certainly distribute her weight more evenly, but carrying her in his arms appealed to the romantic streak in him. It wasn't as though he often had a chance to hold a beautiful woman.

He turned in a semi-circle and pondered his next move. Behind the line of cabins hugging the shore of Lake Huron, was a large, two-story log lodge sitting atop a small rise. Perhaps someone would be there who could help.

As he hiked up the path, he felt the unfamiliar whisper of silky hair against his bare arm. Her scent rose, an odd combination of honeysuckle mixed with sweat, dirt… and the sour smell of fear.

Snakes, she had said. Suddenly he realized that this might not be a simple faint. Perhaps she had been bitten.

He began to run.

He mounted the steps to the front porch of the lodge in two bounds and kicked the screen door so hard it rattled in the frame. He decided that if someone didn't come to the door, he'd break it down. The young woman needed a doctor. He would find a phone and call an ambulance.

"Is anybody here?" he shouted.

A woman who appeared to be in her early forties rushed to open the screen. She was dressed in a flowered blouse belted over what looked to be a long, fringed, buckskin skirt. Her dark hair, sprinkled with gray, was pulled back into two long braids.

She took one look and gasped. "What happened?"

"Do you know this lass?" he asked.

"Of course." The woman's face tightened with fear. "She's my niece. Her name is Moriah. Bring her inside immediately."

As he maneuvered Moriah through the door, all he registered about the place was massive overhead beams, smoke-darkened walls and heavy wooden furniture. An old blue and white quilt, framed and protected by glass hung on the wall.

"Where do you want me to lay her down?"

The woman piled two pillows on the end of a worn, brown leather couch. "Over here."

As he carefully laid Moriah on the couch and positioned her head on a pillow, it was easy to see the family resemblance between the two women. Both had the same high cheekbones, deep-set eyes, and long, dark lashes.

"What happened to her?" the woman asked. "Where did you find her?"

"She came crawling out from under a cabin yelling 'snakes,' and then she fainted. That's all I know."

"It's too early for snakes."

"That's what I thought, but she said there was a nest of them."

"I should probably check for bites, although if she were bitten I don't think the bite alone would make her faint." The woman tugged the tail of her niece's blue flannel shirt out of her jeans and then began unbuttoning it. "Knowing Moriah's fear of snakes, even if she just saw one beneath that cabin, it might be enough to make her pass out."

Ben knew it was an emergency and all, but still... he didn't know what he was supposed to do while the aunt started to undress her. Should he leave? Stay? Turn his back? One thing he was fairly certain about was that standing there staring at them was not what the situation called for.

A blush began at the base of his neck and traveled upward toward his scalp. Sometimes he just hated being a redhead. It made it impossible to have the slightest embarrassing thought without the color of his skin announcing his discomfort to the entire world.

"Don't just stand there," the aunt said. "Pull off her boots."

Grateful to be given a job, he knelt and focused all his attention on unlacing Moriah's well-worn, steel-toed, work boots. Who *was* this girl, anyway? She had a face fit for the cover of a fashion magazine, a body that made him sweat with the effort not to notice, and the calluses of a construction worker. He carefully pulled off her boots and peeled away heavy cotton socks, revealing slender, shapely feet.

"Her skin feels cold and clammy." The woman nodded toward the other couch. "Bring me that afghan over there."

He jumped to obey and brought her the tan and blue afghan that had been lying folded. In his hurry, he tripped and nearly fell over his feet as he approached the two women.

"Goodness." The aunt snatched the afghan away from him. "You're rather a goose, aren't you?"

"Yes, ma'am," he agreed, wholeheartedly.

While he studied the ceiling, the aunt checked Moriah for puncture wounds.

"No bites, thank God," she finally said. "Keep watch over her while I go get a damp cloth from the kitchen."

Ben watched the aunt's long fringed skirt swish against her ankles as she disappeared into an adjoining room. Then he glanced down and forgot all about the aunt. Moriah, covered to her chin with the tan and blue afghan, looked like a slightly worse-for-wear Sleeping Beauty. The pallor that had worried him had left her face. Long, black eyelashes made two perfect crescents against her tanned skin. Parted lips revealed even, white teeth. Hair as shiny as raven's wings tumbled across the pillow.

A streak of dirt smeared her right cheek. He leaned over and gently brushed it away. Her skin felt like velvet.

He was awkward around women and he knew it. Always had been. Probably always would be. Being raised in an all-male household was not exactly conducive to learning how to converse easily with women. High school and college had been relatively painful, except for the academics, in which he had excelled.

Some men, if they were especially handsome, could slide by on their good looks alone—even if their main form of communication was grunts—but he was not a handsome man. Never had been, never would be. Nothing he could do about it. He was the way God created him, and that was that.

Living in the jungle for the past five years hadn't helped his social skills a whole lot, either. When this girl was properly awake, she probably wouldn't give him the time of day. That's just the way things were. Thirty-two years on this earth had given him plenty of time to get used to being overlooked by beautiful women.

Even women who weren't beautiful didn't exactly queue up to stand in line to get involved with a man who spent most of his time sitting in a hut and swatting mosquitoes, while studying the language of a remote Amazonian tribe.

Savoring this stolen moment, before she could regain consciousness, he dared to tuck a strand of her hair behind a perfectly delicate ear. He was so engrossed in studying her, that it startled him when the aunt came striding back into the room. He took a guilty step backward.

"Moriah has not fainted in a long, long time." The aunt knelt and wiped her niece's face and neck with a wet washcloth. "But when she does, it tends to go deep and last long enough to scare everybody to death."

The girl's eyes fluttered open at the touch of the wet cloth.

"Katherine?"

"Yes, dear. I'm here."

"What happened? How did I get here?" She saw him standing there and blinked. "And who are you?"

"He says you found a nest of snakes." The woman refolded the washcloth and laid it again upon Moriah's forehead. "I checked for bites, but you're okay. You don't have any. This is the man who was kind enough to carry you in here a few minutes ago."

"You're the man I ran into on the path?" Moriah pulled the wet cloth away from her face. "I remember now."

"I'm Ebenezer McCain, but you can call me Ben."

"Katherine says you carried me in here?"

"Yes."

"All the way from Cabin One?"

"Actually," Katherine said, "he ran. I was in the front bedroom upstairs and heard you yelling something. The window was open. I glanced out and saw him running up the hill carrying you."

"You carried me?" Moriah's eyebrows shot up. "Up that hill? And you *ran*?"

"I was very worried."

"I'm not small."

He was certain there was something appropriate to say here, but for the life of him he did not know what it was. Instead, he simply fell back on the truth.

"You're a whole lot heavier than you look," he said. "No. Wait a minute. That didn't come out quite right."

Katherine, who had been deadly serious up to that moment, snorted with laughter.

"Thanks—I think." Moriah shifted beneath the afghan. "Can I get up now?"

Ben stared at her in uncomprehending silence for a couple of seconds. Then he understood what she was trying to say. She wanted to get dressed, and all he could do was stand there and stare.

"Sorry. I'll go wait outside…"

He hurried out the door, collapsed onto a rocking chair on the porch, and began to rock nervously. Talking to a pretty girl could sure take it out of a guy.

He stopped rocking when he heard Moriah and Katherine's voices floating through an open window.

"What did he say his name was?" Moriah asked.

"Ebenezer McCain," Katherine said. "He said to call him Ben."

"Ebenezer is a weird name. I don't think I've ever heard that one before."

"I know," Katherine said. "The only time I've ever heard it before was Ebenezer Scrooge from Charles Dicken's *Christmas Carol*."

Seriously? They were making fun of his name? It might sound funny to them, but it had come down through several generations of his family, and he was proud of it.

"I'm supposed to have a cabin reserved here for the summer," he called in through the window.

Silence.

Moriah lowered her voice to a whisper. "I don't remember a McCain on the books."

"Try looking under Bennett," Ben prompted. "That's my employer's name. He told me his secretary made the reservations."

"The man certainly does hear well, doesn't he?" Moriah muttered.

Ben folded his arms across his chest. His first day on Manitoulin Island and things were not going at all like he had envisioned.

For the past month, he had eagerly anticipated spending the summer here. It was the largest freshwater island in the world, and he was grateful for the temporary stonemason job that would replenish the funds he needed to continue his work in South America.

A summer-long respite from the oppressive Amazon heat sounded heavenly. The luxury of having a cabin all to himself with no curious tribesmen wandering through his living quarters day and night, was attractive also.

It was only for two or three months, of course. When he finished here, he would go back to his translation work, but in the meantime, he planned to enjoy every minute of his working vacation. At the moment, however, he was tired and groggy from too much travel and too little sleep, *and* it felt like he had somehow managed to make a fool of himself to boot.

He closed his eyes in weariness. Then a frightening thought struck and propelled him to his feet. Everything he owned in the world was sitting in the middle of the path where he had dropped his luggage in his rush to catch Moriah. He leaped off the porch, ran down the hill, and came to a sliding halt when he reached the place where she had fainted.

His breathing slowed as he saw that his two duffle bags were still exactly where he had dropped them. He knelt, unzipped compartments and reassured himself that everything was intact, including every penny he owned.

He carried his belongings to the first cabin and stacked everything upon the front steps. Then he picked up a rock and strolled around to the side where he had seen a large hole in the cabin's foundation. Unlike Moriah, he had no fear of snakes, but he was curious. He threw the rock into the hole and was greeted by the eerie buzz of rattles.

Chapter Three

"Ben left very suddenly," Katherine said, glancing out of the window. "Do you suppose we hurt his feelings?"

"I hope not." Moriah pulled on her socks and boots. "He seemed nice enough. Did he really run up the hill while he was carrying me?"

"He did."

"I wish I could have seen that. It would also have been nice to have been awake enough to enjoy it," Moriah said. "I've never been carried by a man before."

"If you were awake, there would have been no need for him to carry you," Katherine pointed out.

You could always depend on Katherine to point out the obvious. Her aunt was the voice of reason in their house. No flights of fancy for Katherine. The woman was as steady as a rock.

"That's true," Moriah said. "He said he was going to be here all summer. Do you have any idea why?"

"From what I understand," Katherine hesitated a moment before answering. "He's been hired to work on a special project here on the island."

"What kind of a project?"

"I suppose he'll let us in on the details later if he wants to tell us."

"I liked him," Moriah tied her boot laces.

"He seemed nice enough," Katherine said. "I don't think he'll be the kind of guest who will cause us any trouble. I'll go down to the cabin and help him get settled in if he's still of a mind to stay."

"Why wouldn't he want to stay?"

"Perhaps he dislikes snakes as much as you," Katherine said. "Maybe seeing you come screaming down the path at him might have scared him off."

"I wasn't screaming," Moriah said. "I was running. In fact, I ran straight into him. The man is so strong it felt like I had hit a brick wall. Somehow I doubt that Ben McCain scares easily."

"I think you are probably right on that score. I'll go help him get properly settled in."

After Katherine left, Moriah's mind flashed back to that awful moment when she realized she had crawled into a den of snakes. She gave a little shiver. Her aversion to snakes bordered on an obsession, but she couldn't allow herself to give into it. There was too much work to do! Tourism season was starting and would soon be in full swing. Some of the cabins had been reserved, but there were plenty of drop-ins. To maximize income, she needed to have every cottage completely ready to rent at a moment's notice.

Sometimes she thought about what it might be like to be a tourist coming to Manitoulin Island instead of someone who lived there all year round.

People came to her and Katherine's resort, looked at the freshly-painted cottages, the well-trimmed grounds, the well-maintained boats and motors and had no idea how much work was involved.

Keeping the place up and running with no help but from Katherine was a little daunting at times. People could be hard on things.

Sometimes she wondered what it would be like to have the time to just hang out with friends in the summer instead of having to work all the time. Or what it would be like to dress up and go out to dinner with some nice guy— but that didn't seem likely to happen any time soon. Single, nice guys were in short supply at the resort. Most of the men who came there were married and accompanied by their families. Or sometimes family men would come alone or with a buddy for a few days of fishing. Since the resort was her entire world, her options were limited.

Of course, if she had been bitten today, finding a nice guy would be the least of her worries. Another involuntary shudder rippled through her body. She never wanted to go through anything like that ever again. She unlocked the closet where she kept her grandfather's ancient shotgun. It was her job to get rid of the snakes, but she would do it from as far away as possible.

Chapter Four

. . . .

"It wasn't just Moriah's imagination, was it?" Katherine said. "There really is a den of rattlesnakes under there?"

Wearing her worn leather moccasins, Katherine had startled him by approaching without making a sound.

"No. It wasn't just her imagination," Ben said. "How is your niece?"

"She's fine. Just a little shaken." From a safe distance, she peered into the dark opening. "I wonder what we should do. We can't allow guests to stay in a cabin that has a den of rattlesnakes beneath it."

He glanced up and saw Moriah striding toward them while cocking an old double-barrel shotgun. She was wearing the same jeans, work shirt, and boots that she had worn when she had passed out in front of him in the middle of the path. Her long, black hair was loose and there was fire in her eyes.

"I'll take care of them," she said. "Stand back."

Katherine and Ben stepped away.

She stopped three feet from the hole in the foundation, dropped to her belly, aimed beneath the cabin and released the safety.

"I don't think you should do that." Katherine said.

Moriah glanced up at her. "Why not?"

"Massasauga rattlers are a protected species."

"I don't care." Moriah went back to sighting down the gun barrel.

"I do." Katherine said. "Killing them is illegal."

"For crying out loud, Katherine," Moriah said, irritably. "So don't *tell* anybody."

Ben listened with interest. He couldn't care less about the snakes, but he wondered if Moriah might still be a little too shaken up to have thought her plan through.

"Is there plumbing beneath that cabin?" he asked.

"Yes," Moriah said. "Why?"

"Do you really want to blow a hole in it?"

Moriah hesitated, registered what he was saying, stood back up, and un-cocked the shotgun. "You make an excellent point, McCain."

She broke open the shotgun, slipped the two shells out, and dropped them into her shirt pocket. He noticed that her hands were shaking.

"Are you okay?" he asked.

"No, but I will be," Moriah said. "I'm going to go back to the lodge and take a very long shower to get the snake stink off me. Then I'll try to pretend this afternoon never happened."

"That sounds like a good idea," Katherine said.

"You," Moriah pointed at her aunt, "are in charge of figuring out what to do about those snakes. I suggest you should get in touch with the people who think rattlesnakes should be protected. Maybe those people would like to come get them. Maybe they would like to keep them as pets."

"I'll take care of it," Katherine said.

Ben watched with open admiration as Moriah strode back to the lodge. "Your niece is really something, isn't she?"

Katherine looked at him, then glanced at her niece, and back at him. A worry line appeared between her eyebrows.

"I'll put you in Cabin Ten; our newest. Moriah framed it up last fall and finished the inside work just last week. You'll be our first guest to stay in it. I think you'll be very comfortable there."

"Moriah built all these cabins?" He had never met a woman carpenter.

"She built the three newest ones. My father built the others. Come along and I'll show you where you'll be staying."

Ben hefted his bags off Cabin One's porch and followed Katherine to the last cabin in the row. He was fascinated with the fact that Moriah had built it.

It was a simple design like all the others; one story, two windows in the front. A deck furnished with a small table and two chairs that faced the beach. The cabin was not large, but it was plenty big enough for a single man to live in for a summer.

"Moriah built this all by herself?" he asked.

"Yes. My niece has many skills."

Katherine unlocked the front door, walked in, and flicked a button to make the fireplace roar into action.

"You might get chilly in the night. You can use the gas logs if you want. Our older cabins have stoves that burn wood, but Moriah installed gas logs in the three newest ones. They give off an amazing amount of heat. She likes to update when she can. There's a campfire ring outside. Some of our guests enjoy sitting round it at night when the weather is warm."

Katherine waited quietly while he scanned the inside of his temporary home.

There was a combination kitchen/living area in front, while two bedrooms with a separating bathroom occupied the back. He was pleased to see that one of the front windows had a desk placed beneath it. He would have a view of the lake whenever he worked there. A navy couch and matching overstuffed chair sat against the opposite wall. A Formica and chrome table with four red vinyl chairs graced the middle of the kitchen. The walls in the combined living room/kitchen area were painted a creamy yellow. The place was pristine and perfect.

"I'm going to love it here," he said.

"Moriah will be glad you like it," Katherine asked. "By the way, how did you get here? I didn't see a car."

"I hitched a ride with a trucker from the airport in Toronto; came across the bridge at Little Current. Then I walked part of the way here until someone else gave me a lift."

"So you don't have your own transportation?"

"Not yet."

"Then you may borrow the lodge truck and get groceries tomorrow morning. If you are spending the whole summer with us, you'll need to stock up. If you need anything else, please ask."

"Thanks." He ran a hand over the smooth walls. "This is a really good paint job, too."

"Moriah did all of it." There was a smidgen of pride in Katherine's voice. "She also installed the plumbing and electricity."

"Impressive," he said.

"Yes, my niece is very competent. She has built a good life for herself." Katherine hesitated a moment before adding. "Here on the island."

Chapter Five

Moriah's stomach grumbled. She awoke and peered at the clock. It was four a.m. and she was hungry.

Throwing an ancient, blue, chenille robe over her flannel pajamas, she padded past her aunt's room in search of a snack. As she went down the stairs to the kitchen, she paused on the landing and glanced out the window. Ben McCain's lights were still on.

That was worrisome. There was no television in any of the cabins and no good reason for anyone to be up at this time of night unless something was wrong.

She downed a glass of milk while standing in front of the refrigerator. Then she glanced out of the window again. That light was still on. Could he be ill? Surely he would come to the lodge for help if he were.

Along with television, there were no telephones in any of the cabins either. Their guests tended to prefer it that way. This was supposed to be a basic fishing camp—a place to come and get away from it all. She and Katherine had never pretended to provide all the modern conveniences. What they had was great fishing and a dynamite view of the lake.

She knew they must be doing something right because, during the summer tourist season, they seldom had an empty cabin. Of course, it made things a whole lot cheaper for them to not have to provide entertainment and instant contact with the outside world. If anyone really needed to use the phone, there was one in the lodge.

They didn't have a computer or internet access yet. They might end up being the last hold-outs on the island, but Katherine preferred the old ways and so did she.

A package of oatmeal cookies lay on the kitchen counter. She grabbed one and took a bite, but that uncomfortable feeling that something was amiss at McCain's cabin kept niggling at her. She decided she'd better go check on him just in case.

A pair of rubber fishing boots lay against the wall where she had dropped them earlier. Now, she plunged her bare feet into their chilly depths and opened the door. Cool air struck her face.

Spring nights in Canada were chilly. Some visitors had a problem with adjusting. Maybe that was the problem at McCain's cabin. She didn't know if Katherine had taken extra blankets to Cabin Ten yet. Her aunt had been busy with the laundry when he arrived and might have gotten distracted. There was a good chance that he was cold, couldn't figure out how to turn on the gas fireplace, and didn't want to bother them at this time of night.

She considered taking him a thick comforter, and decided against it. It would look odd, knocking on a man's door in the middle of the night with a blanket over her arm. It could be easily misinterpreted as her hoping for a sleepover. It would be best to simply go check things out before she started trying to fix a problem that might not exist.

The sky was clear and a full moon illuminated the path. Her eyes adjusted quickly as she clumped along the path beside the lake in her rubber boots. She might be afraid of snakes, but walking outside in the dark did not bother her. Manitoulin Island was a safe place. It had very little crime, and Robertson's Resort always felt like the safest place of all to her.

Small, comforting night sounds filled the air as she walked. Lake Huron lapped at the shore. The sound of the lake was a lullaby embedded so deep in her consciousness that she practically breathed according to its rhythm. A young raccoon scurried into the underbrush, leaving a lake mussel, half-eaten on the path.

"Sorry about that, little one," she said, softly. "I didn't mean to interrupt your breakfast." She tossed her half-eaten cookie toward the lake. Raccoons liked cookies. She knew this for a fact. Katherine had once accidentally left an open package of fig bars outside. It was empty the next morning and had raccoon tracks all around it.

When she arrived at Cabin Ten, light poured out from the two front windows. She quietly and carefully mounted the deck steps and glanced in, relieved to see him seated at the desk absorbed in a book instead of shivering in the corner like she had feared. Ben had apparently felt no need to pull the curtains. He had even figured out how to use the gas logs, which were burning nicely. He stopped reading, wrote for a moment, and then focused back on his book.

Relieved, she turned to go back to the lodge. She was half-annoyed with herself for even bothering to come check things out. Back at the lodge, there was a long to-do-list. Morning would come soon enough and she needed to get some sleep if she was going to...

"Did you need something?" Ben asked.

She whirled and saw him standing in the open door. With one foot in the process of descending the steps, she let out a little yelp and fell backward onto the ground, landing flat on her back.

The wind rushed out of her lungs when she hit the ground. While she fought for breath, Ben leaped off the deck and knelt beside her, lifting her into a sitting position.

"Relax, lass, and your breath will come."

The unexpected feel of his strong arms around her caused her to gasp, and her lungs filled. She began to breathe normally again.

"You'll feel better now." His voice was kind and reassuring, and she noticed the hint of a Scottish burr again. The man had a lovely deep voice. She also realized that he was continuing to hold her upright with his iron-muscled arms.

He smelled of soap and sun-dried laundry and some sort of woodsy scent she couldn't identify but liked very much. Suddenly, she wished with all her heart that she had worn something more attractive than a faded bath robe, flannel pajamas and, oh goodness, fishing boots. This was embarrassing. She pushed herself away from him and shoved herself up off the ground.

"I'm fine," she said, brushing off her bottom. "Thanks."

Ben rose and shoved his hands deep into his pockets as though he thought he had done something wrong. She saw confusion flitting across his face in the moonlight.

"It is very late," he said. "Was there something you needed?"

"I didn't need anything. I was up and saw that your light was on. I thought you might be ill or something."

His expression softened. "I should have told you that I often stay up very late. Your other guests probably turn in early, don't they?"

"Those who plan to go fishing before dawn tend to. I'm sorry I disturbed you."

"You didn't disturb me. In fact… I'm still wide awake. I slept a lot on the plane coming here. You could stay awhile if you want to."

"*Excuse* me?" Disappointment stabbed her. A handful of male guests had made the mistake of assuming she automatically came with their cabin. They had never made that mistake again, but somehow she had not expected Ben to be one of them.

"I— I mean," he stammered. "We could sit out here on the porch and talk if you want. It would be nice to have someone to talk to."

Moriah relaxed as he emphasized the word "talk". It was probably close to five a.m. now. She normally got up at six, and falling off a porch tended to wake a person up. She wouldn't be getting any more sleep today.

"I suppose I could stay for a bit."

"May I offer you some—let's see—all I have is water. I planned to get groceries tomorrow. I mean today."

"Water would be nice."

"I'll be right back," Ben said. "Wait right here. Please don't go anywhere."

He ran to fetch the water with a whole lot more eagerness than she thought the situation warranted.

She decided that she wouldn't mind getting to know Ben McCain a bit better. This was a little unusual for her. Tourist season was so intense that she seldom had the time or inclination to get to know her guests beyond a basic professional courtesy.

But there was something about Ben that intrigued her. It wasn't because of anything particularly special about his looks. His hair was sandy red, unkempt, and much longer than it should be. His hands, large, blunt-fingered and calloused, were workman's hands. His face was honest and plain, unremarkable, except for his eyes. As he'd hovered over her at the lodge, she had noticed that his eyes were an unusual shade of blue. They nearly matched the denim shirt he was wearing.

Even hunched over a book, the width of his shoulders had been impressive. Obviously, he didn't spend all his time reading books or he would not have had the strength to run up a hill carrying her. At five foot eleven and a hundred and fifty pounds, she had yet to meet a man capable of making her feel like a delicate flower, but her brief encounter with Ben McCain came close.

Ben was far from movie-star handsome… but he wasn't exactly hard on her eyes, either.

Unfortunately, with the exception of her childhood friend, Jack, she had always been a little awkward around guys. At least when it came to the possibility of dating one of them. The boys in high school shop class had respected her skill with a reciprocating saw, but they didn't exactly invite her to the prom. Of course, it didn't help that she was taller than most of them, and that she had never developed a knack for boy/girl small talk.

She caught herself wondering if Ben was married, and then shoved the thought aside. He probably wouldn't be interested in her after he got to know her. Most men seemed a little intimidated by the fact that she could take a cranky boat motor apart and put it back together again until it ran smoothly. Or that she could fix a leaky toilet all by herself.

What most of them didn't realize was that, if she didn't do the repairs, there was no one else to do them. She *had* to learn to be handy with tools. She just hoped Ben wouldn't be yet another man who would be put off at the idea of a woman who knew her way around a hammer and nail gun.

On the other hand, maybe it didn't matter what Ben thought of her. For all she knew, the man might have a wife and a dozen kids at home.

At twenty-five, she had not once been on a real date and she had no idea how to go about getting one. Being a girly-girl simply was not part of her skill set. Plus, she had no earthly idea how to flirt.

While other girls had been learning how to capture a boy's attention, she'd been fighting to keep her family's fishing resort from falling apart ever since the year she turned thirteen and her grandfather died. She could build, plumb and re-roof a cabin with the best of them, but somehow she'd never figured out the key to making a guy fall in love with her.

Nor had she met one yet that she wanted to. Until—quite possibly now.

Chapter Six

Ben rifled through his freezer for ice and filled two glasses. He couldn't believe his luck. An intriguing, lovely woman was sitting on his porch right now. At least he *hoped* she was still sitting on his porch. He hurried to go outside before she could change her mind.

As the screen door closed behind him, he stopped, stunned at the picture she made in the moonlight. She was absolutely gorgeous as she sat there, long pajama-clad legs propped up on the banister, a pretty blue robe draped around her. She had long, shiny, black hair and it rippled in the moonlight, reminding him of the Amazon River at midnight. She seemed utterly engrossed in the starlight filtering down on them. His heart turned over at the sight of this graceful beauty waiting for him.

Things like this didn't happen to Ben McCain. Beautiful women didn't just turn up out of nowhere in the middle of the night. Getting to spend some time with Moriah would be a nice memory to take home with him when he left.

"Wishing on a star, lass?" he asked.

"Huh?" Fishing boot clad feet came off the banister and hit the floor with a thud. "Nope. I'm wondering how much longer that gutter will hold."

He handed her the glass of water and took the other chair, feeling a little deflated.

"It's a beautiful evening," he offered.

"Yes, it is. No bugs yet." She ran a finger around the rim of her glass. "Black flies get so thick around here sometimes they can blind a bear."

"Oh. Right."

Ben sat in silence, casting about in his mind for a new topic. Discussing black flies and leaky gutters didn't strike him as appropriate moonlight conversation but he wasn't sure what to do about it.

Moriah took a sip of water and glanced at him from the corner of her eye. "Do you have any kids?"

"Who? Me? No."

She nodded. Took another sip. "A wife?"

He had no intention of even thinking about a wife until he finished his present project. His work in the Amazon was primitive, dangerous and all-consuming. Sometimes even *he* didn't want to be there. He had no plans to drag a woman into it.

And yet, his heart swelled with the possibility that Moriah might inexplicably be interested in him.

"No," he said, happily.

"Living with anyone?"

He thought about the seventy plus tribesmen who considered his hut their own personal property and wandered through it for their private amusement any hour of the day or night.

"Not really."

Moriah glanced at him with narrowed eyes.

"What does 'not really' mean?"

His mind raced. He didn't want to get into the whole thing about his work quite yet. It was such a complicated story. Few people could understand why he had chosen to bury himself in the jungle for the past five years. He'd almost given up on trying to explain it.

"Let's just say that I have a lot of friends who make themselves at home in my house."

"Oh."

She appeared to ponder this while they both gazed out at the lake. A thin line of dawn appeared on the horizon.

"I'm going fishing," she announced.

Talking with this woman could give a man whiplash, he decided, as she drained her glass and tossed the ice over the banister. Then she said words that went straight to his heart.

"Do you want to come?"

Chapter Seven

Moriah felt an unfamiliar flutter in her stomach as she stuck one leg into the pair of jeans that she had flung over the chair last night before bed. She already regretted having invited Ben McCain to go fishing with her. There would be chit-chat. She didn't like doing chit-chat. The chances of saying something stupid were too high. There was also the fact that she had things to do. She didn't have time to go fishing with Ben.

Except that she just wanted to.

Standing on one leg with her jeans half on, she stopped and reconsidered. Under normal circumstances she would wear yesterday's work clothes to fish in without a moment's thought and put on fresh ones after she'd finished and showered off the fish smell.

But not today.

She kicked the already-worn pants into the same corner where her giant antique library globe stood. Her bedroom wasn't fussy, but it wasn't plain either. It held only things she enjoyed using or looking at—things like old maps. Her walls were covered with a collection of framed antique maps. Her furniture was dark mahogany, built at least a hundred years ago. An authentic spy glass sat on her window sill. Katherine said that the room reminded her of a ship captain's quarters, but all Moriah knew was that she liked the way her room felt when she was inside of it.

Which wasn't often. There was way too much to do at Robertson's

Resort for her to lounge around in her bedroom.

She pulled her newest jeans out of a bureau drawer. They were a little stiff, but at least they were clean. Then she threw on her best flannel shirt, slicked her hair back into a tight ponytail, ran downstairs to the extra refrigerator on the front porch where she and Katherine kept bait for sale, and then headed out to the small dock.

She was pulling two basic fishing poles and some gear from the locker when Ben came whistling through the early-morning mist. He was wearing baggy, blue jogging pants, flip flops, and a too-tight grey t-shirt that said, "Kiss me! I'm Scottish!" He carried a large backpack in one hand and a giant-sized tube of sunscreen in the other.

"That's an awful lot of sunscreen." She nodded at the yellow tube.

"I burn easily," Ben said. "I go through cases of the stuff."

"But the sun isn't even out."

"It will be." He offered the tube to her. "I'll share."

She shook her head. "I never use it."

A large pair of sunglasses sat on top of his head. He slipped them onto his nose before stepping into the boat and finding a seat.

"Again?" she said, looking around at the mist. "The sun isn't out yet."

"It will be," Ben explained. "I get really bad headaches without them."

"Whatever works." She had dealt with hypochondriacs at the resort before and she was getting the impression Ben might be another one. Based on experience, she doubted he would last thirty minutes without asking to go back to shore. This was a grave disappointment to her. In her opinion, a man who couldn't go on an early-morning fishing trip without worrying about sunburn and headaches wasn't much of a man. Oh well.

She climbed in, settled down onto a seat and jerked the cord to start the motor.

"You sure you want to go through with this?" She jerked the cord.

"I'm sure," Ben said. "I can't wait. I live to fish."

She jerked the cord again.

Ben settled his backpack onto the floor of the boat. "Maybe you should try the choke."

"I know how to start a motor." Her teeth clenched as she gave another mighty jerk.

Nothing.

Ben reached over her shoulder and moved a lever a fraction. "Now try."

She shot him a glance, then gave one more pull. Of course, *this* time it caught and purred like a kitten. Over the years she had developed a theory that some pieces of machinery had a sense of humor and deliberately chose to embarrass the person dealing with them. This was one of those times.

"I've been repairing boat motors since I was twelve," Moriah said. "I do know how to start one."

"I'm sure you do." Ben nodded in agreement.

"I've taken this one apart and put it back together again more than once."

"I don't doubt it," he agreed. "Do you have life jackets on this boat?"

"You don't swim?"

"Not particularly well."

"There are two of them under the seat."

"Great." Ben pulled one out and tried to hand it to her.

"No thanks," she said.

"Ah." He drew his own arms through it and shrugged it on. It was a little snug. "I'm guessing that you *do* swim well?"

"Like a fish."

"What a surprise," he said.

He buckled on the yellow life jacket, then squeezed out a handful of suntan lotion and began slapping it on while she nosed the metal boat away from the dock. They motored into the mist for a few minutes then, a half-mile from shore, she cut the motor and picked up the extra fishing rod. It was an uncomplicated spinner, the kind with which she taught beginners. Ben watched with interest as she baited it.

"You ever fish before?" she asked.

"Some."

She handed him a pole with an already-baited hook at the end. "Try not to hook yourself. Or me."

Ben reached for the pole and inspected the already-baited hook. "My uncle had a saying about this sort of thing."

"About fishing? What was it?"

"My uncle always said, 'Don't ever marry a woman who won't bait her own hook.'" Ben cast in a smooth, flowing arch and began to reel. "He never told me what to do about a woman who baited her own hook *and* mine."

"Sorry." Moriah apologized. "I'm used to beginners."

"That's okay," Ben said. "It never was my favorite part of the sport, anyway."

She got her line ready, then settled back and cast it with expertise. They sat in companionable silence for several minutes as they watched the ripples from the tiny nibbles, baby fish too young to grab a proper mouthful, or mature ones wise enough not to take the entire hook.

"Can I ask you a question?" she said.

"Sure."

"Where are you from?" She inspected her hook. The nibbles had taken a toll. She rebaited and cast again.

"I was born in Scotland—no surprise there—but my father and I moved to Maine to live with my uncle when I was still a wee lad."

"Well then, that answers that."

"That answers what?"

"The bit of accent you have," she said. "It's nice."

"My accent?" He pretended to be surprised. "I have an accent? What accent? I thought I had gotten rid of it."

"Please don't get rid of it."

"If you like it, Moriah," he said, solemnly, "I will try very hard to hang onto it."

She had stopped getting any bites at all. She cast again. "You said you and your dad moved you to Maine. What about your mom?"

"My mom didn't live too long after I was born. That's one of the reasons we left Scotland."

"I'm sorry."

"So was Dad. He didn't do too well for a long time afterward. My father and uncle were far from perfect but they did the best they could to raise me." Ben reeled in his fishing line, checked the hook, and also recast. "I never went hungry and I learned to work. That's more than a lot of people can say."

"True."

"My turn to ask a question," Ben said. "Why was your aunt wearing that buckskin skirt and moccasin outfit last night?"

"You didn't like what Katherine was wearing?"

"I don't care what your aunt wears, but I've never been to Canada before. I was wondering if wearing buckskin is some sort of custom."

"It isn't exactly a custom. Katherine wears it because she works part time at the Amikook Centre at Wikwemikong."

"I have an extensive vocabulary," Ben looked at her with raised eyebrows. "And I speak five languages, but I have no idea what you just said."

"I don't know the meaning of the words. That's just what it's called. Katherine helps counsel and care for elderly tribal people who come to the Amikook Centre. She arranges for various activities, runs the meals on wheels program, checks on them at home if they're sick. That sort of thing. Katherine is one-eighth Ojibwe, so she dresses somewhat traditionally when she's there. It's a comfort to the older ones."

"Then that makes you...?"

"One sixteenth."

"Oh," he said. "Then that would explain your beautiful hair and lovely skin."

Moriah had no idea how to respond to that. Ben, on the other hand, was completely nonchalant about what he'd just said.

In fact, he continued the conversation as calmly as if they were discussing the weather.

"Wikwemikong? What is that?"

It took Moriah a couple of beats before she recovered her voice. It wasn't every day that a man used the words "beautiful" and "lovely" to describe her. She would have liked to savor it, but Ben had asked a question. "It's the unceded First Nations reservation over on the east side of Manitoulin Island."

"First Nations?"

"People used to call them 'Indians' but First Nations people really hate that word."

"I'll try to remember not to use it, then. What does unceded mean?"

"They never surrendered."

"Seriously? They're allowed to do that?

"Canada's native history is a little different than the States."

"Apparently so."

"Can I ask you something else now?" Moriah said.

"Sure."

"Do you have a job?"

Ben choked on a laugh. "You don't mind being blunt, do you?"

"Not usually," Moriah said. "Does that mean you don't?"

"I do have a job."

"And it is…?"

Ben shrugged. "It's complicated."

"Complicated as in 'I'm an international spy' or complicated as in 'I sell drugs to little kids'?"

"Neither!" Ben shot her a glance. "I'm a linguist. I'm translating the Bible into a remote Amazonian dialect. That's also where I've been living for the past five years."

Her heart skipped a beat at the mention of the Amazon.

"Do you like what you do?" She checked her line and added a fresh worm. Something was definitely nibbling at it out there.

"Most of the time. Why do you ask?"

"We've had morticians, electricians, airplane pilots, teachers, truckers, you name the profession and a person who makes their living at it has stayed with us—except for Bible translators. You're our first."

"Well, that's what I do."

"Why?"

"Maybe because I'm good at it?"

"I thought most people who wanted Bibles already had them."

"I wish they did. But that's not the case. There's over seven thousand languages in the world. Around nineteen hundred still do not have Bibles translated into their own language yet. I'm one of the people who are trying to whittle that number down."

"In the Amazon?"

"That's where several of the remaining languages are."

Moriah laid her fishing rod across her lap, rinsed her hands in the lake, dried them on her shirt and digested this information.

"My parents died there," she said.

"The Amazon? I'm sorry." He sounded genuinely concerned. "How did it happen?"

"Dad was a carpenter. He went there one winter to help build a medical clinic. He and my mother died in a plane crash coming home."

"Do you know where the clinic was located?"

"I've asked, but Katherine says the place didn't really have a name. I suppose it doesn't matter anymore."

"I know the country pretty well, maybe I could find out..."

"I doubt it." Moriah's stomach twisted like it often did when she thought about her parents' death. There was a blackness there that she had never understood. Her childhood memories did not go back past age six. "I'd rather not talk about it anymore."

"Okay. What do you want to talk about?"

"You don't look like a Bible translator," she said.

"No? How should a translator look?"

"You should be skinny and hunched over from studying all the time. You have way too many muscles to be a Bible translator."

"You think I have too many muscles?" Her comment surprised him. This lovely woman had noticed how he was built?

"I think that came out wrong," she said. "What I meant is, you look like you are used to working hard. That doesn't fit with sitting around translating the Bible."

"I do work hard." He recast. "Here's the deal, Moriah. Most Bible translators have to either support themselves by working a second job or they have to ask for donations from churches. My father and uncle were both stonemasons and they taught me a trade that I'm good at and that pays well. Every summer, I hire myself out for a few months and do a project or two until there's enough money for me to live on again."

"I sort of do the same thing," Moriah said. "During the winter I hire myself out to a local contractor to help with inside finish work."

"How did you learn to be so good at carpentry?"

"My grandpa was afraid that Katherine wouldn't be able to run the resort alone after he died, so he taught me how to help her take care of it. He bought me a nail apron when I was only seven. I loved following him around."

"Do you enjoy what you do?"

It wasn't a question she'd ever asked herself. Keeping the resort in good repair was pretty much a matter of survival for her and Katherine. It was simply what she did and probably always would.

She shrugged. "It pays the bills."

"The Apostle Paul supported himself by making tents. That's what my stonemasonry is. It's my tent-making job, except, unlike Paul, I haven't gotten beat up for anything yet... although I suppose it has happened to other translators."

"Oh." Her mind had wandered. The fish were not biting. Just the little nibblers. It was probably way too early in the season to go fishing— let alone take a guest, but one could always hope. "Let's go to another spot I've had good luck with in the past. It's rocky. Sometimes they're biting there."

"Could we move closer to that lighthouse?" Ben pointed. "I'd like to get a better look at it."

The mist had evaporated and the sun had burst through. The broken tower shimmered in the distance above the gentle waves of the lake. She gazed at its familiar form. As always, she silently grieved its present condition.

"Are you a lighthouse buff?"

"Not particularly, but I'd be interested in knowing more about this one. How long has it been unattended?"

"Most of the lighthouses were shut down back in the 60s, before I was born."

"Why did they do that?"

"Money," Moriah said. "A solar powered light on a pole was a whole lot cheaper than paying a light keeper and bringing food and supplies to his family."

"So it's been empty all that time?"

"I wish! Vandals came the summer I was sixteen. Outsiders. They stole the special French-made Fresnel lens in the tower. A few weeks later, they returned and broke all the windows."

"You know for sure it was outsiders?"

"Locals wouldn't do something like that."

"This is a big island." Ben said. "I read that at least twelve thousand people live here. Surely one of them could be a vandal."

"No." Moriah shook her head. She knew what she knew. "Locals wouldn't have damaged the lighthouse. The people of Manitoulin Island cherish the lights that ringed our island. The Coast Guard and government... not so much."

"Okay, so locals wouldn't have vandalized it," Ben conceded.

Moriah reeled in her line. No reason to stay here. She started the motor and began plowing through the waves in the opposite direction of the lighthouse.

"Wait a minute," he shouted over the drone of the boat. "Can't we go see it?"

"No." Moriah had no intention of becoming his tour guide to what she considered her private property. At least not right now. Maybe later, after she got to know him better. "We came to fish, not go sight-seeing."

In a few moments, she shut the motor off near a rocky outcrop toward shore. Sometimes there were good-sized perch hiding there. Ben studied the boulders deep in the clear water beneath the boat, then he dropped the pole she had given him and reached into his canvas backpack.

"I don't want to hurt your feelings, Moriah. That's a fine pole for a beginner, but I'm ready to do some serious fishing now."

Chapter Eight

Two hours later, Moriah nosed her boat into the dock, climbed out and tied it. Ben handed her the two rods and her fishing gear. Without saying a word, she stashed the poles in the locker and rinsed her hands off under the faucet her grandfather had rigged to make it easier for guests to clean their fish.

"There's no need to be surly, lass." Ben untied his stringer from the bow of the boat and pulled it out of the water. It was heavy with bass and perch. "I can't help it if I caught more fish than you."

"I'm not being surly." Moriah dried her hands on the back of her still-stiff jeans.

He flashed a grin, and she noticed how white and even his teeth were. Ben had a great smile, even if it was a little mischievous at the moment. Her prejudice against red-heads aside, Ben was becoming more attractive to her by the minute. "You were just fishing off the wrong side of the boat, Moriah. That's all."

"There *is* no wrong side of the boat."

"Sure there is. Tomorrow morning, I'll take your side of the boat and you can take mine."

She watched the fish flip water all over his pants and shoes. "We're not going fishing tomorrow morning."

"Okay. What *will* we be doing?"

"*We* are not doing anything tomorrow morning. I have to get this place ready for the other guests. Trust me. It's going to get really busy around here soon."

"This afternoon, then?" Ben asked. "This evening? Come on, Moriah. I've waited a long time for this vacation. Some companionship would be nice."

"Your fish can keep you company." Moriah glanced again at the large catch. She couldn't remember ever seeing someone as competent with a fly rod.

"They don't smell as good as you."

"I don't smell so good right now, either."

She felt an unfamiliar desire to—to—*flirt*. But she didn't know how.

A little confused by her feelings for this stranger, she turned and started hiking up the hill to the lodge.

"You'd better start cleaning them," she called over her shoulder.

"You'll help, right?" he shouted after her.

"Nope." She started walking backward up the hill. "My grandpa had a saying about fish, too…"

"What was it?"

"My grandpa always said, 'You catch 'em, you clean 'em.'"

With a wave she left him to his work.

As soon as she got inside the lodge, she went upstairs, stuffed her fishing clothes into the laundry basket and stepped into the shower, her mind filled to overflowing with Ebenezer McCain. He was a surprise to her in every way. Who would have thought that a man so fair-skinned he was nearly allergic to the sun, would turn out to be such an expert fisherman?

He had whipped out a featherweight, collapsible fly-casting rod from his backpack that was so state-of-the-art she had never seen one like it. Then he had attached a tiny hand-tied fly that seemed to tickle the fancy of every fish within a hundred feet of their boat. The man was poetry in motion with a fly rod in his hand. She'd been so mesmerized by the sight that she had laid her fishing pole across her lap and simply watched.

She dried off, ran a comb through her damp hair, and began to dress. As she balanced on one foot while pulling a sock on over the other one, she looked out of the upstairs window and saw Ben cleaning fish with the same single-minded concentration she had seen as he had read and made notes the night before. His movements were quick and spare as he dropped one fillet after another into a bucket. He finished, sprayed down the concrete sink, hung the filleting knife back in its place, and looked up at the lodge. He caught sight of her watching and raised his hand in a greeting.

As he climbed the hill, she puzzled over the feeling of familiarity she felt with that particular walk, that solid build. Even his voice sounded faintly familiar. She just couldn't remember who or where she had seen someone so much like him.

"You want fresh fish for breakfast?" Ben let himself into the back door and sat the bucket in the kitchen sink just as she came downstairs into the kitchen.

"Don't you want them?"

"Of course I do, I'm starved. But I don't plan on *cooking* them. My uncle had another saying… if you catch them, and clean them, somebody else has to fry them."

"Oh." She put her hand on her hip. "Your uncle always said that, did he?"

"Always." Ben nodded solemnly. "It was on a framed embroidery sampler hanging in our kitchen."

"Your uncle embroidered?"

"Yes." Ben looked offended. "Do you have a problem with that?"

"Nope. We've had guests who did much stranger things than that."

"Okay. Maybe I exaggerated a wee bit. My uncle didn't embroider, but I *am* very hungry."

"Unfortunately, I don't cook."

"Why not?"

"Katherine does all the cooking."

Ben cocked one eyebrow, silently questioning her statement.

"My aunt and I divided up the chores a long time ago. She does the inside work and I take care of the outside. Cooking is her responsibility. I've never learned."

"Why not?"

"I just explained it."

"You explained a division of labor. You didn't explain why you're incompetent."

No one had ever said such a thing to her before. Quite the opposite.

"I'm far from incompetent and you know it."

"You said you couldn't cook."

"I suppose *you* can?"

"Of course I can, but I was hoping not to. I'm trying to have a vacation here, Moriah."

Despite the sunscreen, Ben was slightly sunburned and was starting to sound a little out of sorts. He was coming as close to whining as a grown man with a deep voice could. She had seen the same symptoms in resort children who had played hard for too long, and had gotten too hungry.

"How long has it been since you ate, Ben?"

His eyes closed as he calculated. "Except for a bag of peanuts on the plane, thirty-six hours."

Moriah was aghast. "I had no idea you were starving."

"Technically, I'm not actually starving, but I don't remember being hungrier."

"Oh, Ben! I'm so sorry!" She grabbed a skillet. "If you give me instructions, I'll attempt to fry those fish."

"In the meantime…" He grabbed a bag of potato chips lying on the counter. "Do you mind?"

"There's cheese in the refrigerator. Go ahead and snack." She turned the gas on beneath the frying pan. "This might take a while."

Chapter Nine

Katherine walked into the kitchen just as Ben and Moriah were finishing their meal. She was wearing baggy blue capris, a white shirt, and a faded grey cardigan sweater. There were no moccasins on her feet—just regular tennis shoes. Her salt-and-pepper hair was in one long braid down her back. Apparently, she was not working at the reservation today.

He couldn't help but notice once again the striking resemblance between the two women. In spite of her everyday dress, and being old enough to be Moriah's mother, Katherine was a very attractive woman. If this was what Moriah would look like in another twenty years, her husband would be one lucky man.

"Goodness!" Katherine exclaimed. "You two have destroyed my kitchen!"

"Yes, we did," Ben said. "But I did manage to teach your niece how to fry fish."

"Moriah cooked?"

"She certainly did. Although, just between me and you..." he glanced around the kitchen, "I think she's a little messy."

Fish bones littered the table, along with an empty bag of potato chips, and two slices of leftover cheese lying on a plate.

"You had a hand in making the mess, as well," Moriah said. "You can't blame this all on me."

"And I'll have a hand in cleaning it up—but my stomach feels a whole lot better. Thanks for feeding me, Moriah."

Katherine surveyed the table. "A well-balanced diet, I see."

"I'll teach her how to cook vegetables tomorrow," Ben promised.

"I doubt that." Moriah reached for a red ball cap hanging behind the back door.

Ben noticed the insignia. "You're a Cincinnati Reds fan?"

"Not particularly." She turned the cap around in her hand to look at the front. "Oh, I see. Nope—it's just something a guest left behind in one of the boats last year. We weren't sure who and they never contacted us to ask for it back. I liked the color."

She slammed the cap on her head and pulled her pony tail through. "I've had fun this morning, Ben, but I've really got to get back to work. There are some porch steps I need to replace today. I don't want a guest to break their leg and sue us."

Ben stood and began dropping fish bones into the potato chip bag. "Thanks for taking the trouble to go fishing with me."

"No problem." She waved as she went out the door.

Katherine watched Moriah bound down the path, and then closed the door behind her.

"I just had a conversation with your employer's secretary," Katherine said. "She told me why you're here. Moriah won't like this. Have you told her yet?

"Not yet." Ben stuffed the trash into the kitchen trashcan and started putting dishes in the sink. "To tell you the truth, until Nicolas Bennett arrives and makes a final decision about what he wants to do, I'm not entirely certain what all my job will involve."

"Whatever Nicolas decides," Katherine swept the remaining crumbs off the table into her hand and dumped them into the trash. "I'm fairly certain it will break Moriah's heart."

"What makes you say that?"

"Because," Katherine glanced up at him while clearing the table. "That's the kind of thing Nicolas does. That's who he is."

"You know him?" Ben said. "I don't understand."

"Nor do I," Katherine grabbed a damp cloth and began wiping the table's scarred wooden surface. "I never did. I have no idea what Nicolas thinks he's doing, but my main concern is Moriah. If you and Moriah develop an affection for one another it will not turn out well. Trust me on this. Please try to stay away from her."

"All she did was invite me to go fishing, Katherine."

"I know, and that is what worries me."

"Why?"

"Because Moriah hates going fishing."

"Seriously?"

"Seriously. It might be recreation to you, but to her it's work. She's taken too many beginners out over the years. I'm afraid she must already like you to invite you to go fishing."

Katherine went to the sink and began filling it with warm water. "I can't bear to see Moriah hurt. Couldn't you try to find another job somewhere else? Maybe you could talk Nicolas into hiring someone from the island to help him?"

"I gave Nicolas my word that I would at least come and check things out for him. I can't leave. Not now. Not until he shows up and we can make some decisions together."

"That's what I was afraid of." Katherine sighed, resigned. "You'll need food. I'll go get the keys to the truck. There's a Foodland in Mindemoya."

"I'm truly sorry that you're upset," he said, concerned. "But I've only been here a day. I barely know your niece. I've done nothing wrong."

"Of course you've done nothing wrong," Katherine said. "You are a decent and good man. But I know who you are and where you came from, and I promise you, this summer is not going to turn out well. Not for any of us."

"Why do you say that you 'know who I am'?" Ben was dumbfounded. "What are you talking about, Katherine? I'm a linguist and a stonemason. That's it. There aren't any dark secrets in me. I am who I am."

"We'll discuss it later on if you stay the summer, or maybe not. I've said too much as it is." Katherine placed the truck keys in his hand. "Fill the gas tank before you return it."

Chapter Ten

It had been a full year since Ben had found himself behind a steering wheel and it felt good. Katherine and Moriah's fifteen-year-old white Chevy truck, however, which was emblazoned with the logo of Robertson's Resort, was shifting a little rough. He slowed down to stop at a stop sign and realized that the brakes were a little mushy too.

This made him feel a little guilty for having taken up so much of Moriah's time this morning. The girl had her hands full trying to maintain the resort with only Katherine's help. It was no wonder that the truck wasn't in the best shape.

As he drove north on Route 551, he noticed a church with white clapboards and a steeple. It was a pretty place and it reminded him of the church where he and his father had attended when he was a child. There were several cars, ladders leaning against the sides of the building, and lots of young people with brushes and paint cans. Apparently, the youth group was in the process of giving the church a little spiffing up. A man with gray hair and beard appeared to be giving instructions to the group.

Ben pulled into the parking lot. If he was going to be spending the next two or three months here, it might be a good idea to get to know someone besides Moriah and Katherine. This active-looking church group appeared to be a good place to start.

The sign out front said, "Tempest Bay Community Church." He got out of the truck and approached the group.

"Can I help you?" The man politely addressed Ben, but did not take his eyes off the youth group. Some had already scampered up the ladders and were enthusiastically slapping on white paint while the others held ladders and shouted encouragement to the ones up above.

"I'm Ben McCain," Ben said. "I'll be staying at Robertson's Resort for the summer."

"I'm Howard Barrister." The man shook Ben's hand, still watching the kids. "Preacher to this group of hooligans as well as their parents."

"Looks like you have a good crop of young ones coming up," Ben said. "Do you think they'll actually get it painted?"

"I'll be happy if none of them fall and break their neck," Howard said. "This was not my idea, but it became my job to make it happen."

Ben noticed that there was about as much paint ending up on the ground and the teenagers as was getting on the building. He sympathized with the preacher's concerns.

"Katherine and Moriah Roberts attend church here most of the time," Howard said. "Nice women. Hard workers. It's not an easy task trying to keep that resort going by themselves. In the past, I've offered to have our youth group go over and help them get ready for tourist season, but Moriah always refuses... politely, of course... but she seems to take a dim view of the idea."

"I'm not surprised." Ben said. "Hey, speaking of her needing help, the resort truck I borrowed needs some work. I think Moriah has been too busy getting ready for the other guests to arrive to tend to it. If I had some tools and a place to work on it I'd do the work myself—but I don't. Do you know of a good garage around here that you'd recommend?"

"There's Denovans down the road if you want, but my house and garage is next door here. I do most of my own mechanic work, so I have plenty of tools." He chuckled. "Working on my car gives me a nice change from trying to get my people to behave themselves."

"Thanks," Ben said. "It's been awhile since I had a chance to get my hands on a vehicle."

"How's that?" Howard took his eyes off the kids long enough to give Ben an appraising look.

"I've been living in the Amazon for a while and I don't leave often. I'm working on a Bible translation for one of the tribes."

"Oh?" Howard ignored the teenagers for a moment. "You said your name is Ben McCain?"

"Yes."

"You aren't, by any chance, Dr. Ebenezer McCain, the Bible translator who has been working with the Yahnowa?"

"Yes." Ben was a little taken aback. "I am, but how do you know about me and the Yahnowa?"

"I have a son who was attending a Bible college a couple of years ago when you were in the States. You spoke at his chapel service. He talked about it for a long time. He was so inspired he thought he wanted to become a translator too."

"Great. Did he?"

"My son?" Howard shook his head. "Nope. It turned out that learning another language took a great deal more effort than what he was willing to expend."

"It comes easier for some than others," Ben said. "It isn't work for everyone. Sometimes I wonder if even I am cut out for it."

"In what way?" Howard asked, obviously intrigued. "I imagine it isn't the translation work that's hard for you."

He liked Howard. The man seemed genuinely interested. Ben was pretty certain this church was lucky to have Howard as their preacher.

"Honestly? It's the loneliness... and getting homesick. When I first arrived, everything was new and different and I was fascinated with the work. Also, I was also buoyed up by the knowledge that I had a gift for languages and that I was doing God's work. I felt like I was in the right place at the right time doing exactly what I was meant to do."

"What happened?"

"Nothing. I'm still working at it, and I will finish the translation, but there are times when the work becomes tedious and I'm hot and itchy and the mosquitoes are driving me nuts and I would give anything just to be able to drink an ice cold Pepsi and watch a movie."

At that moment, over Howard's shoulder, Ben saw a girl in torn jeans accidentally spill part of a bucket of paint on the head of a girl with long, dark hair, who had been holding the ladder beneath her.

"Is that oil paint?" Ben said.

"Yes," Howard said. "Why?"

A scream erupted as the girl with long, dark hair realized what had happened.

"I think you have some spilled paint to deal with. I hope you have a lot of mineral spirits on hand."

Howard turned, took in the scene and sighed.

"No need to hire professional painters, the building committee said. Get the teens involved, they said. Let *them* paint the church, the committee said. It'll keep those kids out of trouble, they said."

The girl with paint dripping off her hair was dancing on the spot, yelping for someone to get her a towel, while the other girl kept apologizing down to her.

"Better see what I can do before that paint starts to dry," Howard said. "I don't think I can send her home like that. Garage is open. Go ahead and help yourself to whatever you need."

"Good luck." Ben did not envy Howard.

"It's okay," Howard said. "The one doing all the screeching is my daughter. I'll see if her mother can help me take care of it."

Ben pulled the truck around to the preacher's garage. He was getting out of it when he heard Howard talking to his daughter as they headed toward the front door. Howard was carrying a half-gallon jug of mineral spirits.

"It's okay, honey," Howard was saying to her. "Don't worry. I think you'll look good in a crew cut. Think how cool it will feel this summer without all that hair."

"Dad!" The girl wailed. "I'm not cutting my hair!"

A few minutes later, Howard came outside and asked if Ben had everything he needed.

"I'm fine, thanks," Ben said. "How's your girl?"

Howard grinned. "Her mom is taking good care of things. Pretty sure my daughter's scalp is going to be pretty raw before this is over though. Now, if you'll excuse me, I think I'd better get back over there before anything else happens."

"That would be wise," Ben said.

As he opened the hood of Moriah's truck, he was grateful for having stopped by. In addition to getting the use of the preacher's garage and tools, it looked like he had found a good church to attend this summer, and was looking forward to it.

He was also looking forward to seeing Moriah's face when he gave her the truck back, all tuned up and ready for the influx of summer guests. She would be so pleased.

Chapter Eleven

Moriah pulled a tape measure across a seasoned oak board, measured it a second time, marked it with a flat carpenter's pencil, and sawed it straight across. Along with the whine of the circular saw, her grandfather's voice rang in her ears.

Measure twice, saw once.

She drilled the oak board three times on each end, selected a nail from her leather carpenter's apron, coated it with a sliver of bar soap, then drove it through to the support board in one expert motion.

A true carpenter can sink a nail with one blow.

It bothered her that she had to resort to soaping the nails and drilling, but that had been a trick of her grandfather's, too, when he was working with well-seasoned, granite-hard oak. The sight of his skilled hands and the sound of his voice while he was working was one of her most comforting memories. He had been such an important part of her life that it sometimes seemed as though he was still with her.

Because of her grandfather's teaching, she was also competent with basic mechanical things like boat motors, but nothing felt as good to her as working with wood. Framing the three new cabins and finishing them out these past three years had meant more to her than anyone could possibly know. There was a lot of satisfaction in building something that was strong and sturdy and, as a bonus, would bring in more income.

She stood and stretched her back as she gazed out toward the lake.

In the distance, she could see the battered lighthouse. Owning and repairing it had been an obsession for as long as she could remember.

The Canadian Coast Guard certainly couldn't be trusted to care for it—even though their name was presently on the deed. They did not have a good record for preserving Canada's lighthouses. Several communities had lost these precious historic landmarks when the Coast Guard dynamited them out of existence in the middle of the night. No warning. Just one-hundred-fifty-year-old historical buildings blown to bits. She could quote dates and locations.

But they wouldn't do that to hers. Not Eliza's Lighthouse. Not if she had anything to do with it. Only one more season with the resort, especially with the extra cabins, and she should have enough money saved for a good-sized down payment.

She was grateful that there had been such an outcry from the Canadian people about the carnage that the Coast Guard had been forced to start selling some of the lighthouses to private individuals instead of destroying them. It was upon this that her hope was fixed. She had been besieging them with letters for the past year, offering to purchase the derelict lighthouse.

It had continued to be unseasonably warm. The sun was beating on her back. It would have been wise not to wear her black work t-shirt. Pulling a blue bandana out of her jeans hip pocket, she wiped the sweat off her face and surveyed her work. The steps on Number Four Cabin were now sturdy and strong. No lawsuits waiting to happen there.

Cabin One needed some small repairs as well, but she was depending on Katherine to make arrangements for someone to come capture and move the snakes first. Whatever Katherine did, it needed to be soon. Only a few more days until the giant ferry boat, the Chi-Cheemaun, which meant the "big canoe", would begin bringing people across Lake Huron to the south shore of Manitoulin. Then tourist season would be off and running in earnest. She and Katherine already had most of the cabins reserved through September.

Nearly everyone came for only a week. It was rare for someone to rent for two. Someone who was renting for the entire summer, like Ben, had never happened at Robertson's resort before. The cabins were expensive. None of the rentals worth staying in on Manitoulin Island were cheap. They couldn't be. It was a matter of survival as those who made their living depended on making enough during tourist season to live on through the winter.

This was going to be a particularly interesting summer with Ben here. She really liked him. Who knew that just frying fish together could be so much fun? It had been a long time since she had laughed so hard. In fact, she couldn't remember *ever* laughing so hard.

As though conjured by her thoughts, Ben came sauntering down the path with a bag of groceries in his arms. He stopped, took a good look at the job she'd just finished, and gave a low, appreciative whistle.

"Those steps should hold for at least another century." His voice held genuine admiration.

Moriah accepted the compliment with a modest nod, but it felt good to have someone compliment her on her work. That didn't happen often. Most guests either didn't notice it or they took the care she gave to the resort for granted.

"Thanks." She felt a glow of pride as she fitted the hammer into the loop on her carpenter's apron. "But I'll be happy if they last for the next five years. People are awful hard on things."

"Oh, and speaking of being hard on things," Ben shifted his bag of groceries from one arm to the other. "Here's your truck keys back." He tossed them to her and she caught them in midair. "Katherine loaned them to me so I could go into town and get some groceries. I stopped at that church down the road where you and Katherine attend and met the preacher. Nice guy."

"We like him," Moriah said.

"Howard and I talked a bit and he offered me the loan of his garage and tools to work on your truck. I picked up some things I needed in town to help me fix the problems it was having. It should run real good now."

"Oh?" Moriah tried to sound grateful. "That was nice of Howard to loan you his tools and garage."

"I added some oil—you were low—and put on new brake pads. You were almost down to the metal."

She didn't know what to say. Truth be told, she *hated* for anyone to mess around with the truck and wished Katherine would quit loaning it out to guests. She was also embarrassed that her vehicle had been a topic of discussion between Ben and Howard. The idea of those two men discussing how she had allowed her vehicle to get into less than pristine shape was embarrassing.

"I also picked up an additive for the transmission. It seemed to help quite a lot. It was shifting a little rough when I first started out."

The tone of his voice told her that he was quite pleased with himself. She started to politely thank him for his help, but he made the mistake of saying one word too many.

"You really ought to keep on top of things like that, Moriah. I know you're busy and all, but your old truck has a lot of miles left in it if you'd take better care of it."

No one had ever criticized her mechanical ability before. There hadn't been one thing wrong with that truck. Had there? She tried to remember the last time she had changed the oil or the brake pads but she couldn't. She had been so busy lately that all her chores had begun to run together in a big blur in her mind.

Ben grinned like a small boy who had brought her a present. She knew he was waiting for her to jump for joy but his mild criticism stung.

"You've certainly been busy," Moriah said, her voice flat.

Ben stared at her, his grin turning into puzzlement. "Are you mad at me?"

"I prefer to take care of my own equipment and vehicles."

Silence.

She glanced up at him and saw that his blue eyes were fixed on her. He cocked his head to one side as though she were a puzzle he was trying to solve.

"I haven't had my hands on an engine in over a year, lass. It felt good to work on that truck. I didn't have anything else to do today and I thought I'd help you out by doing something I know how to do."

She stuffed the rumpled bandana back into her hip pocket. Ben had obviously meant well, but there was always the possibility that he didn't know what he was doing. For all she knew, in his ignorance, he could have damaged something. She really couldn't afford a major repair bill right now. Buying a new truck was out of the question—not when she was socking away every spare penny for a down payment on the lighthouse.

"I know you thought you were doing me a kindness, Ben, but from now on, please ask before you try to fix anything else."

"It's a deal," Ben said. "And from now on, you might try saying 'thank-you' when someone does something nice for you."

"I can't help it if I don't like people messing with my things."

"Seems to me like that's how you support yourself." He glanced around. "By renting out everything you own."

That, of course, was true. She rented out everything from the cabins to the boats and the motors that went with the boats. In a pinch, she had rented out the spare room in her and Katherine's lodge as well as tent space on the undeveloped acreage along the lake. She even rented herself out as a tour guide on occasions. Not to mention picking up odd jobs on construction sites around the island during off-seasons.

She made a dollar any legal way she could and there was nothing wrong with it. Her lighthouse fund was growing daily and that made it all worthwhile.

"There's nothing wrong with the way I make my living."

"No, but maybe you can understand my confusion. I thought the truck was resort property—something you lent out to guests—most of whom probably never bothered to contribute to its upkeep."

He had her there. "Actually, I'm surprised if they even bother to put gas in it."

He waited.

"Okay then," she said, reluctantly. "Thank you."

"You're welcome." Ben walked off toward his cabin.

"How much do I owe you?" she called after him.

Ben stopped, shook his head with disbelief, and kept walking.

Moriah watched his retreating back with regret. She'd done it again. Said the wrong thing. Acted the wrong way.

This is why she enjoyed working with wood and machinery. Wood didn't get its feelings hurt. She never felt like kicking herself after completing a building project. People, on the other hand... well, people were hard.

She heard the screen door on his cabin slam shut as she bent to retrieve her tools. She carefully put each one away in its place in her toolbox, then she temporarily tucked the box and circular saw under the steps she had just built, and made a decision.

Ben had tried to be kind to her this afternoon and, aside from some mild teasing, he had been nothing but nice to her ever since he'd arrived. She really did owe the man an apology. It was a relief to know that her truck was in good shape. She really was grateful, and she doubted he'd made any mistakes in the repairs. Ben just wasn't that kind of person.

She was pretty sure she knew how to make amends for her annoyance with him.

She marched down the path to his cabin, knocked on the screen door and glanced inside. He was in the kitchen area, putting some of the food into the refrigerator. At her knock, he came to the doorway, and leaned against the frame. He wasn't smiling.

"It was a gift, lass. You owe me nothing."

"I know. Thank you." She shoved her hands in her pockets. "I thought you might enjoy going with me to see my lighthouse now. I check on it every few days. You can come with me if you like."

"*Your* lighthouse?"

"Yes."

He remained exactly as he was. Arms folded, leaning against the doorframe. "Is that your idea of an apology?"

She glanced at the light fixture above his head. It needed one of those new florescent compact bulbs that she was replacing the old bulbs with.

"I guess."

He shrugged. "Okay."

Chapter Twelve

Ben marveled at the different moods of the lake. It was nearly as change-able as Moriah. Earlier, in the morning darkness, it had been as smooth as a mirror. Now, it was decidedly choppy. The late afternoon sunlight reflected off the tops of the waves which glittered like diamonds.

He pulled his sunglasses out of his shirt pocket and put them firmly on his nose. He did *not* want a headache while he was with her. It was hard enough keeping up with the woman when he had a clear head.

She looked like a woman on a mission as she steered the boat over the waves, intently focused on getting there. She had explained that going by boat was the quickest way to get to the lighthouse since the Coast Guard had allowed the dirt road leading down the middle of the short peninsula to grow into a small forest. It discouraged visitors, Moriah explained, which was okay with her.

After a few minutes, she beached the boat and, together, they pulled it far enough onto the shore that the lake couldn't reclaim it. Then Moriah climbed the gentle rise and he followed. When they reached the top, Ben found himself on a grassy plateau dotted here and there with rocks, at the edge of which stood a stone light tower soaring above an attached stone cottage.

The keeper's cottage was a story-and-a-half, and it definitely needed work, but the thing that arrested his total attention was the wicked-looking crack zigzagging up the side of the light tower. The tower was nearly eighty feet high and built out of limestone. It was beautiful, broken and dangerous.

Still, the place took his breath away. Even damaged, the tower proudly sat outlined against the blue of the sky and the lake. The cottage, with its matching stones, hugged the tower like a faithful little companion, determined to keep its friend company even if it was badly hurt.

He studied the light tower with the appreciation of a stonemason. It required time and patience to chisel stones into the shapes necessary to build such seamless walls. In spite of the damage, he could tell that a master stonemason had created the place. Such skill was rare—even back in the 1800s when the lighthouse was probably built, but thanks to his father and uncle, he possessed the ability to build as well as the old masters.

Small spring flowers were already tentatively peeking out through the grass. In spite of the damage to the place, the yard area wasn't overgrown.

"If the Coast Guard doesn't bother to keep a road open to the place," Ben asked. Who mows it?"

"I do."

"You drag a lawnmower all the way over here on a boat?"

"No. I keep one here, in the old boat shed down by the lake. That way I only have to bring a gas can with me. It's not much trouble."

"On top of everything else you have to do, you come and mow property that doesn't belong to you?" he said. "Why?"

"Because I love it here." Moriah opened her arms wide and turned in a circle—indicating the whole small peninsula and the lighthouse. "I always have loved it here. And I'll be able to buy the place soon. Katherine and I have saved nearly enough for a good down payment."

Ben froze. "You've what?"

"Saved enough for a down payment. The Coast Guard has begun selling off some of the older lighthouses. I want to keep this one in the

Robertson family if I possibly can."

"I don't understand," Ben said. "I thought you said the government owned most of the old lighthouses."

"They do." Moriah sighed. "At least on paper. But I've always believed there is such a thing as a sort of a moral ownership too. My family took care of this place for over a hundred years. They rescued people from boat wrecks, kept the light shining no matter what the weather was like, and sometimes they kept it going in spite of sickness and death. They lived their lives here."

She pointed to a patch of ground near the front of the keeper's cottage. "In a few weeks, the daffodils that my great-great grandmother, Eliza, planted will blossom here. They are the old-fashioned kind that smell so good. My grandfather always took special care of them, and I do too. One of the men she and her son helped rescue during a terrible storm, sent the bulbs to her. The man said he sent them as a living golden medal for her bravery. There's a picture of her that hangs in the great room at the lodge. Katherine put it beside that quilt she made. She's wearing a high lace collar and her hair is all done up fancy for the photographer. When you look at that photograph, it's hard to imagine her rowing out to rescue people during a storm—but she did it."

"I had no idea they ever let women be light keepers way back then," Ben said.

"There were quite a lot of them over the years. A woman named Ida Lewis was one of the most famous. Her father had a stroke soon after he moved his family to the lighthouse, so Ida and her mother kept the light going. Then her mother got sick. Ida took care of both of them, kept the light going at night, and went out and rescued by boat at least eighteen people over the years. Most of the women light keepers got their jobs under the sort of same sad circumstances that turned Ida and my great-great grandmother, Eliza, into one."

"What sad circumstance did Eliza have to deal with?"

"For Eliza, it was her husband's death. At least they thought he must have died. Liam Robertson disappeared the first winter he was employed here."

"You don't know for sure what happened to him?"

"No. It's always been a bit of a family mystery. From what we can tell, Eliza didn't know either. He just disappeared one night and never came back. It was in the wintertime, and she was snowed in with their son who was just a little boy. There were rumors that Liam went hunting for game because their food reserves were getting too low and he just never came back."

Ben could only imagine how isolated and desolate this place must have felt to a woman alone with a child. "That must have been terrible for her."

"I'm sure it was. Especially since other rumors said that he had grown tired of being cooped up with his wife and son and had abandoned them. All we know for sure is that when spring came he still hadn't shown up, and never did show up, so the government allowed her to stay on instead. Once they saw she could take care of things, they formally hired her. I suppose it was a lot easier than finding someone new and training them. She already knew how things worked. Her son, who was my great-grandfather, eventually took over when he grew up. And *his* son, my grandfather, kept the light going until the government started replacing the lighthouses with electric lights and letting the old light keepers go."

She stood, gazing at the lighthouse with so much passion and love showing in her face that it was almost painful for Ben to look at her. Especially knowing what he knew.

With this trip to see the lighthouse, things had suddenly gotten very complicated for him, and he was not a man who welcomed complications. His work was complicated enough. As she continued to tell him the history of the place, he realized how deeply rooted she was, and it made him feel sick to his stomach.

Nicolas had never told him that there was a girl building her life on dreams of restoring the lighthouse. It made everything so much worse that she was opening up and sharing her dreams with *him* of all people. If he had known the job he had been hired to do would break someone's heart, he would never have agreed to come.

"Wouldn't it take too much work to fix it up, Moriah?" he said, trying to dampen her enthusiasm a little. "Looks to me like you already have your hands full."

"I'm young. I'm strong. I'm definitely not afraid of hard work and I want to do this. I've *always* wanted to do this. It would mean the world to me if I could make this come alive again."

He could easily see all the holes in her plan, but he doubted she could. She had dreamed of this scheme for far too long to clearly see all the problems involved. Unless she and Katherine had a much larger stash of money than it seemed, trying to bring this place back to life would be impossible.

"I'd rather not run over *that* next time I mow." Moriah picked up a stone about the size of her fist and threw it toward the lake. "Sometimes it seems like the earth around here grows rocks like some sort of crop."

Ben knew that she would probably never mow the place again, but he didn't think it was his place to break it to her. But if not him, who?

Instead, of telling her what had happened, he chose to change the subject.

"How did your family end up running the resort?" he asked.

"When Grandfather saw that the Coast Guard was beginning to phase out the lighthouses—it didn't happen all at once—he bought the adjoining property and built the lodge and the first seven cabins.

Tourism had just begun to hit Manitoulin Island, and land was still cheap. He hoped the cabins might provide an income once the lighthouse was decommissioned."

"And did it?"

"Yes, slowly. But the ship captains complained that the battery-operated light didn't show up as well as the old one, so Grandfather and my Dad kept the tower lit anyway on bad stormy nights even though they didn't get paid for it."

Her voice was so proud telling him this. It was obvious that her father and grandfather had achieved heroic stature in her eyes for keeping the light burning.

Katherine had been right. It had been a mistake for him to get to know Moriah because she was definitely going to despise him before the summer was over. It bothered him that apparently Katherine had known what was going to happen, but had chosen not to break the news to Moriah. Why? Did she plan on him doing it? Or had she postponed upsetting her niece while they were still in the middle of getting ready for all their guests. Perhaps she was postponing it until Nicolas's appearance forced her into it.

Moriah walked along in front of him, her long, loose hair rippling like a silken black scarf on the breeze. He could still remember the feel of her skin and the scent of her hair when he'd caught her in his arms yesterday.

Regardless of what Katherine had in mind, he knew he had to tell her. Now. This was the moment and the time. If he didn't break it to her now, she would be embarrassed by the fact that he had allowed her to go on and on about what she intended to do with the Robertson Lighthouse—especially since he knew all along what would happen.

And yet as he watched her now, glowing with enthusiasm, the words to destroy her dream stuck in his throat. She was so beautiful, so strong, and yet so vulnerable. In bringing him here, she reminded him of a little child who had offered to share her favorite toy after accidentally hurting a friend's feelings. There was something decidedly childlike about her, an innocence, in spite of the fact that she was a grown woman. It made him want to protect her, to shield her from hurt. Which made no sense at all. Truth be told, he barely knew her... and yet, in the few hours they'd spent together so far, it felt like he had somehow known her all of his life.

"We had a good year last year." Moriah confided. "So I put in a bid on the lighthouse a couple of months ago. They sent me a letter saying they would give it serious consideration. As far as I know, I'm the only one interested in it. I don't think anyone else would want to take on all the repairs. If they accept my bid, I'll have to mortgage the resort, but we'll be able to handle the payments. Especially if I keep getting winter construction work."

"What would you do with it if you had it?" Ben continued to wrestle with his conscience. Should he break it to her or not?

"I would repair the tower first. Then I'd fix the cottage and rent it out to help pay the mortgage. Lots of people would like to vacation in a lighthouse. I'd also rig up some kind of light after the tower is repaired." She turned and looked at him, her eyes so vulnerable and trusting. "It doesn't seem right not having a light in that tower. I thought maybe if I could find something that would work well, I could come over on bad nights and light it like my grandpa and Dad did. The ships don't really need lighthouses anymore—they use radar systems instead, but I'd like to do it anyway. Even with radar, there are still wrecks sometimes."

Her hopes were so naked and sweet, Ben wished the ground would open up and swallow him before he had to destroy her dream. But the ground didn't open up, and he stood mute while Moriah went on trusting him with all that was in her heart and he gathered his courage to tell her what he knew.

"If I could do that, the sailors would know that there was a real, living person here that cared about them, not just a light bulb on a pole. It might make a difference, you know?"

"It's a wonderful dream, Moriah, but I have to tell you something. I'm so sorry…"

A small, black, pontoon plane appeared in the sky, circled low over the lighthouse, flew away, and then approached again. They watched as the plane made a smooth landing near their boat.

"Who could that be?" Moriah shaded her eyes. "I've never seen anyone come here by plane before."

A head emerged from the cockpit. A fortyish man with a compact build and dark hair unfolded himself, climbed down onto the pontoons and stepped onto the beach. He was neatly dressed in navy pants and a white shirt. With dismay, Ben realized that he knew the pilot.

"I really need to talk to you, Moriah…"

"In a minute, Ben. Right now I want to find out who that is." She strode toward the plane. "If it's someone from the Coast Guard, I need to talk to them."

"Moriah, wait!" Ben hurried after her.

He caught up just as the pilot reached the top of the bluff.

"So, McCain, you're already here," the man greeted him. "Good. I'm glad. What do you think of the place?"

"I think you're a week early," Ben muttered.

"Do you two know each other?" Moriah looked from one to the other.

"This is Dr. Nicolas Bennett." Ben was furious at Nicolas for coming a week early, but there was nothing he could do about it. "He's the one who hired me to come here for the summer."

"Oh, hello," she said, pleasantly. "I'm Moriah Robertson. My aunt and I own the resort where Ben is staying."

Nicolas accepted the hand Moriah offered, held it firmly in both of his, and studied her face.

"You resemble Katherine."

"You know my aunt?"

"Since we were children." Nicolas turned to Ben. "It's getting late. I want to check out my property before it gets too dark. Since you're already here, we can get a head-start on making plans."

"*My*' property?" Moriah's voice quavered. "What's he talking about, Ben?"

"I was trying to tell you…"

"Katherine didn't explain all this to you?" Dr. Bennett asked.

"Apparently not." Moriah put her hands on her hips. "Exactly what is it that Katherine didn't explain?"

"I acquired the land and buildings a short while ago. I engaged Ben to hire a crew to tear this decrepit light tower down before someone gets hurt."

"The cottage, too?"

"Yes. I doubt it's repairable," Dr. Bennett said. "I plan to start out fresh and erect a new house on the site. Now, if you'll excuse us, Moriah, I need to work out some plans with Ben."

Chapter Thirteen

Moriah felt her face grow hot. She could not believe what she was hearing. How could this man, this stranger, own *her* lighthouse? It was unthinkable. It had to be a lie.

"I don't believe you."

"Excuse me?"

"I said I don't believe you."

Nicolas seemed distracted by something. He pulled a small leather-bound notebook out of his pocket and made a note with a slim silver pen. He took his time, while Moriah waited for his response. Finally, he finished writing, closed the notebook, tucked it away, and placed his pen back in his shirt pocket. "Why not?"

Moriah's dislike for the man was growing rapidly. He seemed arrogant and rude, but worst of all he seemed to be under the mistaken impression that he owned her lighthouse.

"Because I've been trying to buy this place for the past two years." She ticked off her arguments with her fingers. "I've been in frequent contact with the Coast Guard, waiting for them to decide to sell it. I've written letters, saved a down payment, applied for a mortgage. I've done everything except sign the final papers."

"Oh?" Dr. Bennett's voice was emotionless. "Well, I signed the papers and paid in cash. Apparently they didn't want to wait for your mortgage."

Tears started to well up in Moriah's eyes, but she forced them back.

She did not know who this man was, or how he knew Katherine, but she was determined not to cry in front of him.

"I was getting ready to tell you, Moriah," Ben said "But Nicolas came too early. I'm so sorry."

"I need to go." Moriah spun away and strode to her boat. She had to get out of there before she broke down. How could this have happened?

As she motored across the water, she was so lost in thought that, instead of coasting in, she accidentally rammed her boat against the dock, leaving a dent in the boat's aluminum bow. Furious with herself for letting that man upset her to the point of damaging her boat, she jumped out and jerked the rope around a post so hard that she got a rope burn on the palm of hand. She needed to talk to Katherine. Maybe her aunt could make some sense out of this mess.

Katherine was hanging sheets on a line stretched between two poles placed between the lodge and the lake. She wore that shapeless gray cardigan over her clothing which, in Moriah's opinion, made her look sixty instead of forty-seven. But that was unimportant. Nothing felt like it mattered now. The one thing she had dreamed of most of her adult life had just been jerked out from beneath her feet.

"Is there something you intended to tell me?" Moriah's throat tightened at the thought of asking her aunt about such bad news. Katherine had wanted the lighthouse as much as she, and had agreed to mortgage the resort if necessary. At least she'd thought her aunt wanted it as badly as she did. "Why on earth didn't you tell me someone had already managed to purchase the lighthouse?"

"Wha…?" Katherine had clothespins in her mouth. Her hands froze in the process of straightening a wet sheet draped over the clothesline.

"I was showing the lighthouse to Ben. Then this strange man arrived and said he had bought it!"

Katherine's eyes widened as Moriah's words tumbled out. She waited for her aunt to explode with indignation and mirror her own outrage, but instead, Katherine merely paled, removed the clothespins from her mouth, and finished pinning the sheet. Her hands were shaking so badly she could barely complete the easy task.

"I didn't expect him to come so soon." Katherine's voice was low and tense. She lifted the empty laundry basket and held it tightly against her side. "He's here a week earlier than his assistant said. How did he get here? I didn't hear a car."

"Pontoon plane." Moriah stared at her aunt, confused. "Why does it matter how he got here? Are you telling me you actually know this man? This Nicolas? And you never bothered to mention him to me?"

"I hoped to never have to tell you about him."

"Even though you knew he was coming?"

"I hoped he would change his mind," Katherine said. "Nicolas does things like that… change his mind at the last minute."

If Moriah thought she was confused before, she was completely at a loss now. Why was Katherine acting so weird? She had never seen her aunt so flustered and upset.

"I have to leave." Katherine clasped the empty clothes basket and whirled in a circle as though unsure of where to go. "I need more time. I need to get out of here. I can't bear to face him yet."

"What is *wrong* with you?" Moriah asked.

"I just need to leave, Moriah. Right now."

The sound of a plane motor coasting through the water made them both turn toward the lake. As it nosed in beside the dented boat, Ben jumped out and tethered it to the dock.

Nicolas Bennett pulled himself out of the plane, carrying what appeared to be a black leather overnight bag with him.

"Look at that," Moriah pointed out. "Carrying an overnight bag. How presumptuous. Do you suppose he actually expects to stay here?"

Katherine stood as still as death as Nicolas approached her.

"Katherine?" Nicolas's voice sounded tentative and hopeful. The impatience he had shown with Moriah was gone and in its place was a man filled with what seemed to be a sort of awe.

Katherine didn't respond, or even move. Moriah had never seen her aunt look so upset.

"It's been such a long time." Nicolas dropped the black satchel and held out his arms as though reaching for a hug.

Katherine took an involuntary step back.

When the hug didn't materialize, he picked his satchel back up and said, "You look well, Katherine."

Moriah was stunned to see tears glide down her aunt's cheeks. Katherine was the most stoic person she had ever known. Not once had she ever seen her aunt cry. Never.

Not until this moment. What had this man *done* to her?

Katherine pressed her knuckles to her lips as she backed away. Then she dropped the laundry basket and fled toward the lodge's parking lot. As the three of them watched, she climbed into her ancient brown Ford Taurus and sped away, leaving behind a cloud of dust.

Moriah realized her mouth was hanging open and shut it.

She'd never seen Katherine run away from anything. Her aunt was upbeat when money was short—which was nearly always—and had patched up more accident-prone tourists than Moriah could count. She faced everything straight on without flinching. The Katherine who Moriah thought she knew would have given Nicolas a piece of her mind and then shooed him off if she felt he needed to be shooed off.

Nicolas shook his head, as though in sorrow, hefted his satchel and wearily trudged back to his plane while Ben stayed behind with Moriah.

"Do you have a clue what that was all about?" Ben asked.

"None." Moriah's world had just shifted on its axis. "Do you?"

They watched as the plane roared to life and taxied far out into the lake before taking off. "Where do you think your friend is going?"

"I have no idea. I'm not even entirely sure I want him as a friend—not after the way Katherine acted."

The pontoon plane had barely disappeared when a second cloud of dust rose from the end of the driveway and grew denser as a van neared the lodge. It was filled with what appeared to be a very large family. When she saw who it was, her heart sank. They had such terrible timing.

"It's the Kinkers from Michigan." Moriah told Ben, exasperated at their sudden, unannounced appearance. "That's just what we need right now."

"Moriah," a large blonde woman trilled, waving through the open window of the front seat. "We're back!"

Moriah glanced at Ben and shrugged. "Excuse me, but I've got to go to work now."

Happy shouts filtered out to them as four small towheaded boys piled out of the van carrying fishing rods, beach balls and luggage. The assorted debris of a family who had traveled many hours tumbled out onto the ground, completely unnoticed by anyone in the van.

"The boys were so excited about coming we just couldn't hold them back any longer, so Farley closed down the shop and we came a little bit early. I knew it wouldn't matter. We've stayed here so often I feel like we're as close as family. Can we have our usual cabin?"

Ben and Moriah watched Camellia Kinker struggle to get out of the van. She was a thin, tall, blonde, and appeared to be at least nine months pregnant. Moriah sighed. This could get complicated.

She made a quick calculation. Although she usually put the Kinker family in Cabin One, the cabin closest to the lodge, the rattlesnake problem hadn't been addressed yet. From sad experience, she knew that the Kinker boys were too curious and undisciplined to be put in such close proximity to a den of rattlesnakes, although she felt a twinge of pity for the rattlesnakes.

"I think we'll put you in Cabin Nine, Camellia. It's one of the new ones."

"Don't you charge extra for the new ones?" Farley Kinker was a tiny man whose head barely reached his wife's shoulder. Moriah often felt, looking at him, that the exuberant and often clueless Camellia and their four rowdy children had somehow drained all the life out of him. There seemed to be nothing left to him except a constant hum of worry about expenses.

"Not for loyal customers like you," Moriah said.

"You'll put that in writing?"

"I'll put it in writing, Farley."

Having the Kinkers arrive first thing in the spring was actually a good thing, she supposed. It always helped her appreciate the guests who came later.

"I don't care where we stay." Camellia kneaded the small of her back. "Just get me to a bathroom."

Chapter Fourteen

....

After Moriah had deposited the Kinker family in Cabin Nine, she gathered all the trash that had fallen out of their van and threw it in the garbage. She took some pleasure in her decision to put them in the cabin next to Ben. It would serve him right to have this chaotic, noisy family next door. She knew it wasn't fair to be aggravated with him, but he should have told her this morning why he had come here. Instead, he allowed her to be blindsided by Nicolas's sudden announcement.

Before returning to the lodge for the evening, she carefully blocked off the hole beneath Cabin One with cinder blocks. Last summer, the Kinker boys had spent the biggest part of a week beneath Cabin One's porch, accompanied by any food they could sneak out of the lodge's kitchen when she and Katherine weren't looking. She shuddered, thinking of the possibility of one of them crawling beneath the cabin before something could be done about those snakes.

By the time she finished getting the hole blocked and the Kinkers settled, the sun was setting and she was exhausted. The day had started at four in the morning when she felt compelled to go check on Ben. It had been filled with a rollercoaster of emotions, including the devastating news about the lighthouse and Katherine's strange behavior when Nicolas came to call.

The worse thing was that, as full as the day had been, the only productive thing she had accomplished was rebuilding those cabin steps.

Everything else involved getting acquainted with Ben, going fishing with Ben, fixing breakfast with Ben, taking Ben to the lighthouse...

The lighthouse. The Kinkers had been a momentary distraction but now the realization that it was lost to her came flooding back into her heart. Without the exciting goal of bringing the lighthouse back to life, the future looked like nothing more than years of summers with her and Katherine going about their routines, waiting for the tourists to show up, and years of winters hiring out for indoor carpentry work.

She knew she should be grateful for her life—and she was—but the lighthouse had given her something truly wonderful to look forward to. Some people saved up for their vacations all year long. That seemed to put an extra bit of excitement into their lives, but she already *lived* where other people came to vacation. She wished she had a dollar for every time some guest told her how lucky she was to live on Manitoulin Island.

What exactly was it that Nicolas said he was planning? If she remembered right—and she was dealing with shock at the time her mind was whirling—it sounded like he planned to tear everything down and build some sort of a vacation house on top of the original foundation... or something like that.

She went to the back side of the lodge porch, the side that faced the lake, and sat down in her favorite porch chair—a split hickory rocker that felt as comfortable as an old sneaker. The view of the sunset was magnificent from this vantage point and nearly always soothed whatever troubles she had.

Tonight, however, the setting sun merely illuminated the view of the lighthouse she had cherished since childhood. She was angry, but she wasn't even sure who to be the angriest at. The mortgage company in being so slow to approve her application? The Coast Guard for selling the lighthouse out from under her? Nicolas for scooping it up from right under her nose.

Or should she be angry at herself for allowing herself to believe that her love for the place gave her some sort of special claim. She should have pushed harder for that mortgage. Paid closer attention. Instead, she'd concentrated on scraping together enough money all while day-dreaming about how wonderful it was going to be to own it.

Funny. She had never dreamed someone from the outside would come in and steal it away from her. The lighthouse had always felt like it belonged to her—a broken down guardian that would someday come alive again. Making enough money to secure it legally had been the focus of her life ever since she was old enough to understand what that ownership needed.

As the sun sank beneath the lake and darkness settled in, she bit her lip in an effort to hold back the tears, but the sharp pain didn't help. If Nicolas had truly purchased the lighthouse—and she had no reason to doubt that he had—there was nothing she could do about it. No legal recourse.

With no one around to hear, she finally gave in to grief over the death of her dream.

* * *

Ben was investigating the boat dock to see if he had left his sun-glasses there. They were his best pair and he had misplaced them. Then he heard Moriah's quiet sobs and forgot all about his sunglasses and pretty much everything else on his mind.

The lodge was completely dark. She hadn't even turned on any lights. Katherine's car wasn't in the parking lot, so Moriah must be all alone... and crying.

He wanted to go and try to comfort her, but intruding on her pri-vacy might upset her even more than she already was. After all, they didn't really know each other all that well yet. He didn't know whether to intrude or not. Still, he suspected that it took a lot to make Moriah cry. Listening to her sobs was breaking his heart. He wished he could do something that would help.

He tried to ignore the sound as he headed back to his cabin, but it just wasn't in his nature to walk away from someone in pain. He turned around and headed back toward her even though his head continued to debate with his heart the wisdom of approaching.

Personally, he could not care less about the lighthouse. In his eyes it was, after all, just a pile of rocks. There was nothing sacred or eternal about it. He had the expertise to tear it down and build another just like it if he wanted to. In fact, with enough time he had the talent and skill to make an even better one. Tearing down the lighthouse was nothing more than a job to him… except for the fact that he would be tearing Moriah apart with each heavy stone he took from it. Even though he'd only known her a day, he already cared about her. He didn't want to cause her any unhappiness.

He approached quietly then, when he got to the porch, he stood for a moment and watched. She didn't seem to know he was there. Her legs were drawn up against her chest, her arms wrapped around them, and she sat with her forehead pressed against her knees. Her whole body shook as she wept.

He quietly walked over to her, knelt down in front of her and put his hands on the arms of her rocker.

"Moriah?" he said, softly. "Is there any way I can help?"

Startled, she jerked upright, her legs flew out, and she kicked him square in the chest.

Surprised and in pain, Ben suddenly found himself sitting on the porch floor, legs splayed.

"Ben!" Moriah exclaimed. "What are you doing here? You scared me to death."

He rubbed his chest where she had kicked him with her steel-toed work boots. Hanging around Moriah was most definitely not for sissies.

"I heard you crying. I wanted to see if there was anything I could do?"

"Oh." She wiped her eyes with the back of her hands. "Okay."

He pulled a handkerchief from his back pocket and offered it.

"It's clean," he said. "I think."

"Thanks." She accepted the handkerchief and blew her nose. "I'd rather be alone right now, Ben. If you don't mind."

"You don't have to talk to me." He dragged a chair over and sat down beside her anyway. "I just came to keep you company."

"I don't need any company."

"Maybe *you* don't, but I certainly do," he said. "It's been a rough day."

"You've got the Kinkers next door. You could go keep them company. Go talk to them."

"I think they're pretty busy talking to each other at the moment. That family makes more noise than any group of people I've ever been around. Even the littlest one goes around screeching, apparently just for the fun of it. Or maybe so he can get noticed. The other three just argue with each other most of the time. Farley yells at them from time to time but they pretty much ignore him."

"Do I need to put you in a different cabin?" She gave a soft laugh, then hiccoughed from having cried so hard. "Are they too loud for you?"

"No. They aren't too loud. I'm used to noise. The jungle is never quiet. In fact, I'd place the noise that the Kinker boys make somewhere between a tree full of frightened monkeys and a puma's growl. I have learned to sleep through both of those. But, if they bring out some drums and start banging on them, I might have a little difficulty. Drums are really hard to sleep through. Trust me on that."

"You're serious?" Moriah sniffed and blew her nose again.

He was pleased to see that, not only had she stopped crying, she seemed to be somewhat interested in what he was saying, so it seemed to be a good idea to keep talking.

"Well, truthfully, I still have a little difficulty sleeping through a puma's growl. My hut isn't all that substantial. Where I live sometimes feels... a little unsafe."

"Are there snakes there?"

He nodded. "Big ones."

"And yet you still plan to go back?"

"I have to."

"Why?"

"It's in my DNA."

"What do you mean?"

"I made a promise." He shrugged. "And I keep my promises. It's kind of a thing with McCain men. At least it was with my dad and my uncle. They didn't make promises quickly—they always gave it some thought first—but once they made a promise, they kept it."

There was a long silence as Moriah digested this.

"So, how did Nicolas and you get together? How did he even know how to find you out there where you were living?"

"That's easy. He's a doctor. He came to help the people I'm working with. We met there and got to know each other. It had nothing to do with who or what I am."

She released a shuddering breath, the kind that comes after a hard cry. Ben heard it and knew that the storm was over—at least for now.

"Nicolas doesn't seem to be the type to do charitable work," she said.

"That's what I thought, but he told me that, now he's retired, he's looking for something to do with his time. Some way to give back. I got the impression he doesn't quite know what to do with himself. At first I thought he might be one of those people who just thinks working in the jungle with a remote tribe is romantic."

"Is it?" She turned in her chair to look at him, fully engaged.

"Is it what?"

"Romantic. Do you enjoy living in such an exotic place?"

"At first it felt romantic and exotic. Plus there was the extra joy in feeling like I was doing what I was meant to do. In the beginning everything was new and different. It was all an adventure. But not so much after the first hundred mosquito bites. That and the heat can kill off the romance of the place pretty quick."

"You didn't take mosquito repellent?"

"Of course I did. Quarts of the stuff. But those insects get so hungry the repellent doesn't always work as well as the labels claim. Plus, did I mention it's hot? Pretty easy to sweat the repellent off."

Ben hoped he'd managed to distract her away from the subject of Nicolas with his tales of mosquito woe, but he hadn't.

"What made Nicolas go after my lighthouse? Do you have any idea what brought him here?"

"He said he had lived there when he was small."

"That's very odd," Moriah said. "He appears to be about Katherine's age. If he stayed here, he would have known my father and aunt, but I've never heard her mention him. She never said anything about another child living here with them. My grandfather never mentioned it, either."

"I don't know anything except the little I just told you. He stayed with me a couple of weeks. I don't have the most comfortable living conditions, but he never complained. While we worked together, he mentioned that he was considering buying a lighthouse on an island in Canada, but he said it was in really bad shape. When he discovered that I supported myself as a stonemason, he showed me a picture and asked if I had the skill to disassemble the stones and incorporate them into a new dwelling. I said I might, but I needed to inspect it on site first. The next thing I knew, a few weeks after he left, he sent word that he had bought it and that he had made arrangements for me to come here for the summer."

"Why did he choose to show up to work with your tribe?"

"His mother was responsible for having a small medical clinic there. He wanted to see it. He didn't know I was a stonemason until he got there. I think that might have triggered his desire to tear down the lighthouse and do something else with it."

"So, I remembered exactly what he said after all." Moriah rose from her seat and began to pace. "He's planning to tear everything down and just build a house there."

"Not entirely. There are some beautiful stones in that tower that can be salvaged." Ben hoped he could calm her down. "He's already had an architect draw up some basic plans. He's hoping to incorporate those old stones into the new place. I've seen the plans and they're nice. If you weren't so emotionally attached, I think you could see the wisdom of what he is doing. At least he's going to do something good with the old stones. He's not planning to allow them to be trucked off, or tossed into the lake."

She sat back down in the chair and began to rock rapidly. "You don't understand, Ben. You didn't grow up seeing that lighthouse from your window every morning of your life. It always made me feel… safe. Even back then I longed to see a light in it each night."

"Look, Moriah." Ben placed a steady hand on the rocker's arm to slow her down. She was rocking so violently, he was afraid she would rock herself right off the porch. "If it means that much to you, I won't do it. I'll ask Nicolas to find someone else to do the job. That will slow things down considerably because, trust me, he won't find someone to replace me easily. Good stonemasons don't grow on trees."

"You would do that for me?" She stopped rocking and looked

straight at him. As he looked into her eyes, it hurt him to see the weariness and pain there. "What about your DNA and all that talk about keeping promises?"

"I made a promise to the Yahnowa people and to God. I promised that I would bring them a copy of the New Testament in their own language. Barring death, I will keep that promise. I never promised Nicolas that I'd take on this job. All I promised him was to look at it and give him an estimate. I can always find another job. It's no big deal to me to refuse this one—especially if it's going to break your heart."

"You were going to give him an estimate?" Moriah sighed. "I can only imagine what it would be."

"The place is dangerous, Moriah. You do know that, right?"

"You're talking about that big crack in the tower?"

"It's hard to miss."

"I know. It keeps widening every winter. I've been so worried. I wasn't sure what to do about it. Stonework isn't one of my skills. I'd hoped to hire someone—but didn't know for sure who to choose. I don't think any of the stonemasons I know would want to tackle it."

"Anyone with any sense would blow it up and start over," he agreed.

Her eyes blazed at him. "Don't say that!"

"Sorry," he said. "I was thinking out loud again. I need to stop doing that."

"Can I ask you something?" Moriah said.

"Of course."

"Let's suppose I *did* own it and I hired someone like you to fix it."

"Okay."

"How much would it cost to restore it? Give me a ballpark figure."

"But you don't own it," he pointed out. "And I don't think Nicolas is going to give it up."

"Humor me," Moriah said. "I'm just curious."

"I can't say exactly. I know what my time is worth, but I'd also need heavy equipment and a work crew."

"I know that," Moriah dismissed it with a wave of her hand. "But what would have to be involved to bring it back to its original condition?"

"The lighthouse would have to be completely dismantled, the stones numbered, a new foundation poured and then rebuilt, stone by stone. The damaged stones would have to be replaced. My best guess is that it would probably cost way more than you could ever save up no matter how many extra jobs you took on each winter. Depending on how much labor costs on this island, a million dollars would be a very low estimate."

There was a quick intake of breath as Moriah took this in. Then she turned and stared out at the lake in the direction of the darkened lighthouse. He could easily imagine her as a young girl, orphaned by a plane wreck, drawing comfort from it. Possibly even then dreaming of bringing it back to life.

"So you are telling me," Moriah's voice dropped. "That even if I already owned it, I could never afford to repair the place properly."

"Probably not. Not unless you and Katherine have a small fortune tucked away somewhere."

"We don't."

"Do you own the resort outright?"

"Yes."

"And yet it still doesn't seem like you're making a good living off of running it. Since you were going to have to mortgage the place to buy the lighthouse, my guess is that there is a very good chance you might have lost the resort. Things always cost more than you expect—especially when you're restoring and building."

"I don't know what we would do if we didn't have the resort."

"Look, lass," he said. "Nicolas isn't such a bad person, he was very kind to the Yahnowa people he helped, but he is sad. His wife died awhile back and they never had any children. He strikes me as someone who doesn't know what to do with himself. He says some of the happiest moments of his life were spent out on that peninsula. I've seen the plans he had drawn up. The new structure he wants built with the stones won't be an eyesore. I can promise you that. Once you get used to all the changes, you might not even be aware that he's there."

"Oh, I'll know he's there," Moriah said. "And Katherine will know, too. I have no idea what happened between those two, but whatever it was, I think it's pretty obvious that it wasn't good."

Chapter Fifteen

Moriah had a restless sleep, and awoke to an early spring drizzle. The morning was so overcast it hardly seemed worthwhile to get out of bed. The gloom that filled her bedroom matched her mood.

The wooden floor felt damp and chill after she slid out from under her blankets. She shivered, dug into her dresser, and pulled on some heavy woolen socks.

In spite of what Ben had told her the night before, the sick knowledge that she had lost the chance to save the lighthouse her family had tended for generations clouded everything.

She ran her fingers through her tangled hair. Then she walked over to the most precious thing in her room—the giant, waist high globe of the world that sat in a wooden stand taking up one whole corner. She had bought it two years ago from one of the antique shops in town. It had been a great extravagance, but she had seen it, been mesmerized by it, and bought it within minutes of entering the store. Next to the tools her grandfather had left to her, it was her most prized possession.

Katherine had appreciated the globe's beauty as well but, when she suggested keeping it in the main room of the lodge, Moriah had balked. She wanted it where she could study it all she wanted to, with no one to see or think it odd.

Sometimes, she played a private game with it when she was feeling down. Like now. She closed her eyes, gave the globe a spin and put a finger lightly upon it, feeling it glide beneath her touch as it spun. When it stopped, she peeked beneath her finger. Greece. That would be a nice place to go. It was probably warm and dry in Greece. Maybe she would go to Greece someday.

Thinking about going someplace besides Manitoulin Island was a fantasy in which she often indulged. Some people were afraid of heights. Some were afraid of speaking in public. Some had a great fear of being alone. Her problem—much, much, greater than her very reasonable fear of snakes—was her inability to leave the island.

She had fought it, prayed about it, tried to read up on ways to overcome it, but it was what it was. The thought of leaving the island made her knees weak and her heart palpitate and she hated herself for it.

This weakness, this inability to leave the sanctuary of Manitoulin Island, was her greatest shame and her deepest secret. Only Katherine knew.

It was at the root of why she had bought the globe. She kept thinking that maybe imagining herself in all those faraway places might someday help give her the courage to leave the island. At least thinking so kept the hope alive that she could overcome her weakness someday.

She glanced in the mirror and did a double take. Her eyes were swollen from her meltdown last night. Greece forgotten, she headed for the door. She had much work to do before more guests arrived.

Coffee would help. Some very strong coffee. Maybe an aspirin or two. Then a long, hot shower. Then what she needed was a heart-to-heart with Katherine—if she could find her.

Her aunt had not come in last night. That was not particularly unusual. Katherine had many friends on the island. Some of them were elderly with no relatives to help care for them. If there was sickness, Katherine would sometimes stay with them for several days, spending the night and helping the best she could. She seemed to have quite a knack for knowing what to do when someone was ill.

Moriah hoped it was a medical reason that kept her aunt away last night, but Katherine's behavior around Nicolas yesterday had been so odd that it undermined her faith in her ability to understand her aunt at all.

She shuffled down the staircase still in her flannel pajamas and heavy socks, momentarily forgetting the fact that the Kinkers had arrived the night before. The minute her feet hit the bottom step on the stairs, she heard four little voices arguing.

"It's my turn."

"No, it's *my* turn!"

"I had it first."

"Nuh-uh, I'm telling Mom.""

Silently, she backed up the stairs, one step at a time. Since it was raining, Camellia and Farley had apparently sent the children over to play in the lodge's great room where there was a collection of board games as well as a small library of paperbacks that had been left behind by guests. Rainy days often found half a dozen tourists reading or playing games and visiting together by the fireplace.

But usually not at six-thirty in the morning.

Her heart sank at the thought of having to deal with the Kinker boys today. No matter what project she got into, they would be underfoot and into everything. As parents, the Kinkers were... interesting. They did not believe in discipline of any form. Therefore, the boys were only slightly better behaved than monkeys. She was definitely not in the mood to deal with them right now.

A stair tread creaked beneath her and she froze. If the boys heard that she was up, they would be on her like a pack of wolves.

Then she heard the door to the lodge open.

"Hello? Anybody home?" It was Ben.

A quartet of young voices greeted him.

"Hey, mister, you wanna play checkers?"

"Well, I, umm…"

"No!" One of the boys shouted. "Not checkers! I want to play Clue!"

"Clue and checkers are for dummies," the oldest yelled. "I want to play chess."

"Well," Ben said reluctantly. "I guess I could probably play one board game."

Moriah heard him close the front door of the lodge behind him and begin discussing game choices with the boys. Grateful for the reprieve, she quickly retraced her steps to her room, grabbed her blue robe and ducked into the bathroom. Her priorities had changed. A shower first… while Ben babysat the Kinker boys. Then maybe, after she had dressed, she would go check on that coffee. Ben could probably use some as well as herself.

Chapter Sixteen

Forty minutes later, hair dry, dressed in a fresh work outfit of jeans, gray t-shirt, work boots and a black and red plaid flannel shirt, Moriah came downstairs feeling ready to face the day. The scene she found in her great room surprised her. No board games were spread about. Instead, four little boys of varying ages were grouped around Ben as he sat in the middle of the dark leather couch.

The two littlest were on either side of him, cuddled up against the big man. The two biggest perched on a footstool nearby. All were big eyed and engrossed, while he told a story that seemed to involve an inordinate amount of growling.

He was wearing faded jeans and a dark, rust-colored sweatshirt that went well with his red hair. The sleeves were pushed up. His hair was still so wet that she could see the furrows his comb had made as he slicked it straight back. It was too long, and curled behind his neck. His blue eyes danced with good humor as he entertained the children.

As though knowing she was watching him, he glanced up. Their eyes met, and he smiled a greeting that was so filled with warmth that she felt it all the way to her toes.

No man had ever affected her that way before.

Befuddled by her reaction to him, she turned to go into the kitchen and accidentally walked straight into the closed door.

"Ouch!"

"You all right?" Ben asked, concerned.

"Yes." She rubbed her nose. "I need coffee."

"Obviously."

He chuckled and returned to his story.

While she hunted for coffee filters, she found herself rubbing her hip from the fall she had taken off his porch yesterday morning. It occurred to her that she might have a few more bruises and bumps before the summer was over if she didn't hurry up and get used to having Ben around.

Katherine nearly always had the coffee started by six a.m. but Moriah could not find the filters anywhere. Apparently, Katherine had chosen to put them in an odd place.

After giving up on coffee filters, Moriah swallowed the two aspirin she had been promising herself, and wandered back into the great room nursing a glass of orange juice.

Ben had finished his story and the boys were begging him for another.

"Don't you think it's time for breakfast?" His voice held a hint of desperation.

The boys looked at Moriah with hope in their eyes.

"Nothing cooking here," she said. "But your mom and dad might be awake by now. Go see if they can fix you something."

The boys shot out of the lodge.

Moriah and Ben glanced at each other as the sound of a slammed door reverberated through the air.

"You think they're hungry?" Ben asked.

"It's been my experience that the Kinker boys are *always* hungry." Moriah sat down beside him. "Don't worry, Camellia manages to feed them, even if she doesn't believe in disciplining them. Thanks for keeping them occupied while I pulled myself together."

Ben gave a great stretch, and happened to leave his arm on the couch above her. "Are you feeling better this morning?"

"Some. You did get through to me last night about the financial realities of the restoration project, but I'm still not at all happy about what Nicolas has planned."

"I couldn't sleep for a long time last night," Ben said, "And I got to thinking about something. I came over this morning to discuss some things with you."

"You mean you didn't just come over to babysit the children?" She pretended to be shocked.

"As fascinating as the Kinker boys are, no, I did not come to babysit. I've been thinking about the job."

"What about the job?"

"If I do decide to work for Nicolas—and I'm not saying that I'm going to—I'll need a crew. You happen to know the skilled labor on this island and could steer me toward the people we could depend on to do a good job. I could also really use your carpentry expertise when we start to build. That's an area I'm weak in."

The idea had no appeal to her. In fact quite the opposite. She was hurt that Ben would suggest such a thing to her.

"This resort will be filling up with people soon." She shook her head. "It's almost more than Katherine and I can handle under normal circumstances. I'm just not interested."

"Maybe you and your aunt could hire some help?" he suggested. "One thing I know is that Nicolas is planning to pay really well."

"How can he?" Moriah said. "You said he's retired, but if he and Katherine were children together, he's still twenty years or so off of normal retirement age. He couldn't have accumulated that kind of money just being a doctor could he?"

"I got the impression that his wife was the one who had the serious money," Ben said. "I'm guessing he inherited."

"I wish I knew where Katherine is." She glanced around. "She didn't come home last night."

"Should we be worried?"

"I don't think so. At least not yet. I think it might have been her day to work at the Amikook Centre. I'll call her workplace when it opens up. If she's not there, then I'll panic."

The sound of a plane landing in the lake filtered into the lodge.

"Well my goodness. Nicolas's here. How lovely," Moriah said, dryly. "What are you going to tell him?"

"I'm going to give him my professional opinion." Ben shoved his fingers back through his hair. "I just haven't decided exactly what that will be yet. I've not yet been able to inspect the place as thoroughly as I need to. I've only had been able to take a glance at it so far."

Most of their guests had fallen into the habit of simply walking into the lodge during daylight hours, but Nicolas knocked. When she opened the door, he stood stiffly on the porch wearing black dress pants, black wingtip shoes, and a gray silk shirt. She wondered briefly if he had also dressed in business attire while working with Ben with the Yahnowa.

"May I come in?" he asked.

Moriah held the door open. "Of course."

"Ben." Nicolas nodded an acknowledgment as he stepped inside.

"Nicolas," Ben acknowledged.

Silence filled the room.

Moriah pulled her red ball cap off a peg on the wall. "If you'll excuse me, I have work to do."

"Please don't go," Nicolas said.

Moriah stopped and waited.

"I owe you an apology," he said. "I wasn't entirely truthful yesterday. I did know someone else was trying to close on the property. I deliberately undermined the bid. What I did *not* know until I arrived here yesterday was that I had taken the lighthouse away from Katherine's niece."

"Katherine knew about this?"

"I'm not sure. Katherine and I have not spoken for many years. I didn't want our first conversation to be over the phone. I had my secretary call to make arrangements for Ben. I think she might have mentioned the fact of the purchase to Katherine, but I'm not sure." Nicolas glanced around the room, "By the way, where is she?"

"I haven't the foggiest."

"I'd like to speak with her."

"I think it was pretty obvious yesterday that she didn't want to talk with you. Looked to me like that's why she left—to get away from you. She still hasn't come home." Moriah shoved the cap on her head and pulled her ponytail through the back. "How do you and Katherine know each other, anyway? If you spent part of your childhood growing up with her, why hasn't she ever mentioned you before?"

"I'd rather not talk about any of that right now," Nicolas said. "Not until I've had a chance to speak to Katherine."

"Whatever." Moriah turned on her heel, annoyed with all the secrecy.

"Moriah," Ben said. "Please wait a minute. Nicolas and I planned to go back to the lighthouse today. I would appreciate it if you would go with us. Will you?"

"I have work to do." She rifled through a drawer and came out with her favorite pair of work gloves.

"Please, Moriah. You know that place better than either of us. There might be questions you could answer that we need to know."

She hesitated

"I tentatively offered Moriah a job this morning," Ben explained to Nicolas. "You'll need a good carpenter to accomplish what you are planning and she's first-rate."

Nicolas stared at her. "I don't believe I've ever known a female carpenter before."

There might not have been an intended insult behind his words, but the surprise in his voice made her feel like some sort of oddity. Why was it surprising that a woman could create things with wood and nails?

"She's worked with several contractors on the island," Ben interjected before she could respond. "I've seen her work. In fact, I'm living in one of the cabins she built. She's good."

"When you were small," Nicolas said. "I could never have imagined that you would become a carpenter and builder."

"You knew me when I was a child?"

"You were a beautiful little girl," Nicolas said. "And everyone loved you. Including me. Please accompany us out to the lighthouse today. I would consider it a great favor."

Moriah weighed her options. She really did have an awful lot to do. For one thing, she'd hoped to patch the roof on Cabin Four. Mentally, she calculated the odds of keeping the Kinker boys off the ladder. Zero to none. The drizzle had stopped, and the sun was out, but rain was still in the forecast. It wouldn't be wise to be on the roof if another downfall started. She could probably put the job off for a day.

Besides, if her beloved lighthouse was to be torn down, it didn't seem right to abandon it. Like a dying loved one, she felt that she needed to be there, no matter how painful the process might be.

"I'll go," she said. "And I'll take the boat. You two can ride with me if you want. Seems like a plane is a bit unwieldy for such a short trip."

Chapter Seventeen

As Moriah pulled away from the dock, Ben glanced back at the pontoon boat.

"Is the cockpit locked?" Ben asked Nicolas.

"Yes, why?"

"Oh, nothing." Ben mentally wiped his brow in relief. He had just had a vivid mental image of the four little Kinker boys flying off into the sunset.

The view, as they skimmed across the lake, reminded Ben of a Dresden plate he had once seen, all blue and white. Blue lake, blue sky and white clouds. In the distance stood the white limestone light tower. The only thing that spoiled the beauty of the day was Moriah's total silence as she piloted the boat. He could only imagine all the things going through her mind.

She beached the craft and jumped out into the water before he could move. Ben felt silly sitting there while she hauled the boat onto the beach. Nicolas calmly stepped out onto the dry sand as though he were used to other people taking care of him.

"I would have done that," Ben whispered to Moriah as they approached the bluff.

"Why should you when I am used to it?"

Ben shook his head in exasperation as they climbed the rise. He wasn't particularly knowledgeable in the social rules between men and women, but he was fairly certain Moriah wasn't playing by them. If he ended up taking the job and staying the summer, he wondered if there was a library on the island with a book he could read that would give him a clue as to how to go about dealing with her. He was good with books. But being raised in an all-male household had left him fairly clueless about women.

He was also good with stone. Very good. As they approached the lighthouse, he forgot the emotional tempest surrounding him and surveyed the structure with a critical eye.

A portion of the roof on the cottage sagged. Slate tiles were missing from the roof, blown away and scattered nearby. All the windows had been smashed out of both structures. The front door of the light keeper's cottage hung from one hinge. A large, square room connected the cottage to the tower, and an entire corner of it was missing.

"How did all this damage happen?" He gestured toward the gaping wound in the side of the single room connecting the light keeper's cottage to the tower.

"This was where they kept the steam-powered foghorn," Moriah said. "Some local boys tried to start it a few years ago just for the fun of it. They didn't know what they were doing and were nearly killed by the explosion. They ended up in the hospital. That's what caused the crack in the tower, plus most of the other damage. I started to try to fix what I could, but a government official who was inspecting it told me to stop. He said they did not want civilians in here. He said they would do what repairs were necessary."

"Let me guess," Ben said. "They never did."

"No," Moriah said. "They didn't. The official didn't say anything about staying away from the outside of the place, so I just tried to keep it mowed enough that the trees and weeds didn't take it over. I knew if I ever managed to buy it, I'd have my hands full with the inside repairs. I didn't want to have to take a bulldozer to the grounds to get to it."

"Well," Nicolas said. "Since the government has relinquished title to it, I believe we have the right to inspect it. Let's go see how bad it is inside."

Moriah entered through the ragged opening and Ben followed, hoping nothing would fall on his head. Nicolas trailed behind.

Except for the damage to the roof nearest the foghorn room, the cottage seemed fairly intact. Moriah led him through it, explaining the various rooms and what they had been used for.

"This kitchen was built large," she explained, "so the early keepers could use it to preserve the food they had to grow in order to survive. Otherwise they were forced to depend entirely on a ship they called a light tender. Its primary purpose was to bring them supplies in the early years. The problem was, the light tender couldn't always get through the ice in the early spring for those keepers who chose to winter in the lighthouses. That first winter Eliza and her son nearly starved because the boat couldn't get through and it was too far for them to walk out without risking freezing to death before they could get help."

"How did they survive?" Ben asked.

"My grandfather told me that some of the villagers got so worried they hired a man with a dog sled to take her some food that they donated. Even though she had always been a city girl, the next summer she taught herself how to grow a huge garden—which she preserved for the following winter just in case such a thing ever happened again."

"Desperation can give a person the determination to do things they never thought they could do before," Ben said.

"Exactly," Moriah said. "That was the winter her husband disappeared. She never knew for sure what became of him. Since she had nowhere else to go, she asked the government for the job as light keeper and they gave it to her. She tended the light for many years."

"Alone?" Ben asked.

"Not entirely. She had a young son who learned to help her. He stayed on and cared for the light when she no longer could do so. I think there might have been an assistant at one time, but I'm not sure."

"There was an assistant," Nicolas said. "The man with the dog sled who came helped out in the summer months and made a living with his dog sled in the winter. I think he and Eliza might have married at one time. I'm not sure."

Moriah looked at him, questioningly. "How would you know that?"

"I spent a great deal of time here. I paid attention to the stories. I'm probably as familiar with the lore of your lighthouse, Moriah, as you."

Moriah's expression softened, slightly. Ben was grateful to see the change. Perhaps the knowledge that Nicolas wasn't a complete outsider would help alleviate some of her disappointment.

The living room was about half as large as the kitchen. A potbellied stove stood in the center. Its chimney pipe had dislodged from the wall and a pile of soot lay on the floor. Old, pink and green flowered wallpaper hung in strips.

"Was this their only means of heat?" Ben had never been inside of a lighthouse before.

"There is a fireplace in the keeper's office, but there are none in the sleeping rooms upstairs. Katherine said they were frigid in winter. That quilt of Eliza's we keep on the wall in the lodge is the only one that survived. Katherine said she made others, but most of them were worn out from helping keep her family warm for many winters here."

The office was directly off the living room. A fireplace dominated one wall and a huge, scarred, built-in oak desk dominated another. A few uninvited visitors had gouged their initials and dates into the wood.

"This desk is the only furniture left," Moriah said. "It was built into the wall and was too large to fit through the door. Everything else got auctioned off by the Coast Guard when they shut the place down."

"It's a shame," Ben said. "Someone put a lot of time and skill into that desk."

"I was a studious child." Nicolas ran his hand over the surface. "I worked way harder than I needed to. I often did homework here. I remember your grandfather building up the fire in the fireplace in here for me so I wouldn't get chilled. If I had a lot of homework to do, it wouldn't be long before your grandmother would come in with some hot chocolate for me. They were always so kind..." Nicolas's voice drifted off. Then he seemed to gather himself. "Oh well. The past is past. Let's go upstairs now."

Moriah shot a questioning glance at Ben. The sadness and longing in Nicolas's voice was a revelation to both of them.

"How do we get upstairs?" Ben asked.

"The staircase is over here." Moriah disappeared into a small door.

They followed her up a narrow, spiral staircase, emerging moments later into what appeared to be an empty attic that had been divided into two large compartments. The walls were covered with a thick, brownish wallpaper. The partition still consisted of raw, un-milled lumber.

"The theory was, one side for the girls, one side for the boys. That took care of any size family," Moriah explained. "Sometimes the light keepers would need to rescue people from shipwrecks and they would stay here too, men in one room, women in the other, until it was possible to get them home. The light keeper and his wife slept in the bedroom on the main floor."

Nicolas wandered over to a low beam and carefully ran his hand over it as though searching for something.

"Are you looking for something?" Moriah asked.

"I carved my name into this beam when I was a boy. It's still there." He smiled and shrugged. "Childhood memories. Nothing important."

"Okay," she said. "I have to ask. Why were you staying here?"

"My mother and your grandmother were great friends," he said. "They grew up together on the island."

Ben faded out of the conversation. Moriah and Nicolas could figure out family connections without him. His only interest was in the structure and whether or not it was reparable. He glanced out of the window at the light tower. "Is there a way into the tower from the house?"

"Yes," Moriah said. "Through the foghorn room."

"Will you show me?"

"Of course."

Together, the three went back down the stairs to the outside and inspected the large crack in the tower.

"It keeps getting bigger each winter," Moriah said. "Water gets into it and freezes and the rocks pry farther and farther apart."

Ben backed several steps away and gazed up. "Why is there a portion of the top missing?"

"Fire," Moriah answered. "Someone started a fire in it after the Fresnel lens was stolen. I've never understood why someone would want to destroy something so beautiful."

"Some people build. Some destroy. Some do nothing at all." Nicolas said. "I prefer those who build. I've had my architect draw up some preliminary sketches of the house I plan to put here. I have enough sentiment for this place that I'd like to incorporate as many of the stones as possible."

Ben saw Moriah's face grow pinched at the mention of tearing down the lighthouse again.

"It can be fixed," Ben said.

"What do you mean?" Nicolas frowned. "I didn't think that was an option."

"We could salvage the stones and build something else with them, but frankly, Nicolas, it seems a shame."

"What are you suggesting?"

"The cottage isn't in too bad a shape. Mainly it's just water damage. Besides needing to install double insulated windows, most of the rest is cosmetic. I could rebuild the foghorn room and finish out the attic. Repairing the light tower will be a challenge, and expensive, but it can be done. If you wanted to, you could probably make the money back that you spend on repairs by charging admission for people to go to the top of the tower. Put some telescopes up there. Tourists are always looking for some place different to go see."

Nicolas turned to Moriah. "What were your plans for this place?"

"I wanted to restore it, of course." Moriah said. "Rent it out. Maybe live in it someday."

"No," Nicolas dismissed her plans with a shake of his head. "I mean, what had you thought to do in the way of restoring it? Were you going to take it back to the authentic lighthouse in which Eliza lived? Replace the foghorn? Live with oil lamps?"

"No," Moriah said. "I had planned to turn the foghorn room into a large study/bath combination. With dormers, the attic could be made into two large, conventional bedrooms. I would leave the ground floor bedroom, living room, office and kitchen alone except for updating everything. It would have to be gutted, wired and plumbed. Electricity would need to be brought in."

"And the tower?"

"Ah. That I would want to take back to the original design. Repair it, of course. I wish it was possible to still buy an original Fresnel lens, but it isn't. They are much too rare. Most are either in museums or private collections. Instead, I had planned to check into getting some sort of large spotlight for stormy weather. I'd hoped to install a good quality telescope for clear nights. Manitoulin Island has almost no light pollution, so it's an ideal spot for amateur astronomers."

"Could it be finished by autumn?"

Ben's gaze flew to Moriah's face. She was stunned. It took her a couple seconds to find her voice.

"Excuse me?" she said. "What exactly are you saying?"

"All I need is a place to retreat to from time to time," Nicolas explained. "I do not have many friends so I do not need a lot of space in which to entertain. If both of you think it can be restored and repaired without anyone getting hurt or killed in the process, that's good enough for me." He turned away, as though dismissing them both, and studied the view, deep in thought, his hands behind his back.

Ben saw Moriah's continued wide-eyed look of surprise and he wanted to make certain he was hearing what he thought he was hearing.

"Are you serious, Nicolas?" Ben asked. "Instead of tearing everything down and rebuilding, you want me to restore this place based on Moriah's ideas?"

"Yes." Nicolas was engrossed in the horizon and didn't turn around. "Moriah, you will take your work orders from McCain. I'll share the oversight of the repairs until I can see if you are competent enough to be entrusted with the work. Inform Katherine that I'll require the use of one of your cabins whenever I fly in. I shall require one for the entire summer. Tell her she doesn't have to talk to me unless she wishes to do so."

Ben saw her eyes cloud over and knew there was trouble brewing behind them. He knew why. Nicolas sounded like a general giving commands to an underling.

"I appreciate the fact that you won't be tearing down the lighthouse, Nicolas." She removed her cap, pulled her ponytail holder off with one fluid motion and let her hair swing free. "And we do have space for one more summer-long visitor. But I have a resort to run. It takes all my time. I'm afraid you'll need to find someone else to do the job for you. I have my own business to run. As for Katherine… whether or not she talks to you is her business. I don't intend to be giving her messages from you."

She headed back to the boat, her stride as athletic and sure as a gymnast. She was so beautiful and strong. Ben's throat went dry just watching her, but he wanted to wring Nicolas's neck. You didn't talk like that to a girl like Moriah.

"Was it something I said?" Nicolas said, surprised. "After all the drama yesterday when I arrived, I thought she would be delirious with my decision. I thought I was being kind."

Ben dragged his attention away from Moriah. "Did you have servants or something when you were growing up, Nicolas?"

"No. Why?"

"You sure do sound like it sometimes when you talk to people."

"I don't understand."

"Moriah would love to be part of bringing that lighthouse back to life, regardless of who owns it. But she's a skilled craftsman. A person of value. My advice to you is to never talk down to her again."

"Don't be ridiculous," Nicolas said. "Good paying jobs aren't all that plentiful on the island. She'll come around. In the meantime, hire whomever you wish."

"No," Ben said. "I'll hire the workers Moriah recommends to me. I don't know the people on this island. She does."

Chapter Eighteen

....

The three of them rode back to the pier in silence. Each deep in their own thoughts. After Moriah docked the boat, Nicolas asked to borrow it to go back to the lighthouse. She wasn't happy about lending it to him, but he said he needed to search for a special pen that had dropped out of his pocket while they were exploring the place.

Depend on Nicolas to have a pen that was so special he needed to go retrieve it. Moriah had never had a pen she gave a second thought to.

"I wish you hadn't done that," Ben grumbled as he and Moriah entered the lodge.

"Done what?"

"Turned Nicolas down." He dogged her footsteps as she went into the kitchen.

"I told him the truth," she said. "I do have a lot to do."

"You're cutting off your nose to spite your face. You know that?" Ben said. "You know you're itching to be part of bringing that lighthouse back to life but you're too proud to work for him."

"You're right. I don't like Nicolas and I don't want to work for him."

"You don't have to like someone to work for them. If I had to like everyone I worked for I'd be broke and homeless."

"As opposed to what?" she shot back. "Living in the middle of nowhere in a hut?"

"That's unfair, Moriah," he said. "I could have a house if I wanted to.

I could have a very nice house. There is a difference."

"I apologize, Ben," Moriah said. "I respect what you do and I appreciate what you just did back there when you convinced Nicolas the lighthouse could be repaired. Unless Nicolas changes his mind, you've spared me the heartache of watching it destroyed. But why is it such a big deal to you for me to be part of this project? After all, it's Nicolas's lighthouse. Not mine. I already *have* a job and I'm way behind in it."

"Look, Moriah. I'm a stone worker and a translator. I build things. I translate things. Stone upon stone. Word upon word. That's what I do. That's who I am. *You* take boards and nails and make something strong and good with them. I thought working together would be nice. I thought we could make something together that we could both be proud of. But evidently I was wrong. Go ahead and do whatever you want."

"That's been my plan all along." She grabbed a pile of folded towels lying on the kitchen counter, and headed toward the door.

Ben stepped in front of her. "I'm not finished with this discussion. Where are you going?"

"I'm going to take these towels to Cabin One for your boss."

"You can't be serious. You're putting him in the cabin with the rattlesnakes?"

"I'm sure he'll be fine."

"You're kidding, right?"

"Yes. The idea's tempting, but no, I'm not going to put him in Cabin One. He'll stay in Cabin Eight, on the other side of the Kinkers. Perhaps he and the boys will bond. At the very least, they should provide him with hours and hours of entertainment."

In spite of his irritation with her, the idea of the emotionally remote Dr. Bennett staying next door to the Kinker children, made Ben laugh.

"I have to admit," he said. "That would be interesting."

"I get my kicks where I can," Moriah said. "Why in the world that man ever decided to become a doctor is beyond me. I thought people who wanted to be M.D.s needed to actually *like* people and want to help them. He seems so... cold."

"Sometimes it is the people who feel things the deepest who have the hardest time expressing themselves. I saw great kindness in Nicolas when he came to my village. There's more to him than you give him credit for."

The front door to the lodge slammed.

"Help!" a child's voice yelled. "Somebody help!"

"What's wrong?" Moriah ran into the great room with Ben directly behind her.

"My mommy's sick!" The oldest Kinker boy grabbed the sleeve of her flannel shirt and tugged, "Come quick."

She whirled, shoved the clean towels into Ben's hands and ran with Ben following close at her heels.

Farley Kinker emerged from his cabin the moment they clattered onto the porch. His sparse hair was standing on end.

"Camellia's gone into labor, but something's wrong." Farley wrung his hands as he talked. "She's never had trouble having babies. But this time there's something different happening. She's having terrible pains."

"How long has this been going on?" Moriah asked.

"She didn't feel so good this morning," he said. "That's the reason we sent the boys to the lodge. She thought maybe we'd have a new baby by the time they came back."

"Why didn't you take her to the hospital?" Ben asked.

"It's an hour away. Besides," Farley glanced at Moriah, "you know how I feel about hospitals."

"How does he feel about hospitals?" Ben asked Moriah, his arms still stacked with linens.

"Farley doesn't like them, or doctors. They cost too much."

"I vote we drive Camellia to the hospital," Ben said. "Right now. How about it, Farley?"

"She'll be fine." Farley set his jaw and shook his head. "This one is just a little harder than the others, that's all."

"I wish Katherine was home," Moriah fretted. "She would know what to do. She always knows what to do."

"Where is she?" Farley asked.

"I don't know, but I'm hoping she's at work by now. I'll make some phone calls."

Ben and Farley stared at each other for a long minute, while the child who had come for Moriah danced a nervous jig between them. Ben knew next to nothing about childbirth. The closest he had come to it was hearing moans from a neighboring hut and then watching as a tribal woman stepped out with an infant in her arms.

At that moment, a high-pitched scream came from inside the cabin and three scared little boys ran outside. Farley blanched. Ben felt a little light-headed.

"About that hospital thing..." Ben began.

"Mommy says for you to come back inside *right now!*" the littlest boy commanded.

Farley gave Ben one wild-eyed look and then shuffled into the cabin like a man going to his execution.

"Hey, mister. You want to play checkers?" the oldest boy's voice quavered, trying to be brave. "Or maybe tell us another story?"

He looked down and saw that all four children were grouped closely around him. Two were leaning against his legs and gazing at the open door from which loud moans now emerged. The youngest vigorously sucked his thumb and stared up at Ben with wide blue eyes.

Ben didn't know how long this birth process was going to take, but he figured the best use of his time would be entertaining these four little boys until it was over. One thing he could not do was overrule a man about what was best for his wife. With all his heart he hoped Moriah could reach Katherine. Or someone else who knew what they were doing.

"Is there a Monopoly game at the lodge?" he asked.

"Yes!" four little voices chorused.

"Then go get it." He might not have any experience in birthing babies but he did know that Monopoly would take a whopping long time to play. The least he could do was keep the children out of Farley and Camellia's way until whatever it was that would happen, happened.

In moments, the boys came running back with two of them fighting to carry the board game at the same time. It was an old set and the cardboard box was coming apart. Pieces and cards dribbled out of it as they ran.

"Whoa. You're losing things," Ben called.

"I told you so, dummy!" one of them said, smacking one of his brothers.

"You!" Ben used his deepest voice and pointed. "The one who just hit his brother. Go back to the lodge and pick up everything the two of you dropped."

Don't have to," the child said, in a sort of sing song. "Can't make me."

"That's right," Ben's voice was calm. "You don't have to and I can't make you. On the other hand, you can't make me play a game with you, either."

"Go on, do what he says," the younger brother said.

Grudgingly, the boy sauntered back up the path, picking up game pieces and sticking them into his pockets while giving Ben dark glances over his shoulder.

A loud moan pierced the air and Ben winced. He wished he could do something for the poor woman, but keeping the boys out of her and Farley's hair was the best he knew to do for now. That and pray—which he was fervently doing.

While he and the three other boys waited for the fourth one to finish retrieving game pieces, he also heard the sound of a car practically flying over the gravel driveway. With a rush of relief, he saw it was Katherine. Moriah came running out of the lodge. They spoke for a moment and Moriah gestured toward the cabins. Katherine reached into the backseat of her car and emerged with a large, blue tote bag.

"Now what, mister?" the oldest boy said, his task completed. "Where do you want us to play?"

"Inside my cabin," Ben said, distracted by Katherine's arrival. "Go set the game up on the kitchen table. I'll come in a moment."

The children skipped happily into the cabin they had formerly been forbidden to enter.

"Can you help her?" he asked, as Katherine and Moriah strode past him, women on a mission to the Farley's cabin.

"I have no idea," Katherine's said. "I'm not a midwife, but I do have some basic knowledge. My main objective is to override Farley and get an ambulance here whether he wants one or not."

"Thanks." Moriah took the clean towels out of his arms. "We might need these."

Ben watched with admiration as the two women mounted the porch steps. In his opinion, something like that took real courage. He wondered how many other crises they'd dealt with over the years with various guests.

"How are we doing, Camellia?" Katherine called out cheerfully as they entered the Kinker's cabin. "I hear we're going to have a baby today."

Chapter Nineteen

Moriah had seen her aunt in action many times before. As a teenager, she had often accompanied her to the island homes where she ministered to various people who needed her. Even though Katherine was not a nurse, she seemed to know more about dealing with various health issues than anyone Moriah had ever known.

Some of the people on the island spoke about Katherine with awe. They said she had magic in her fingers and that she could draw pain away by her very presence. Moriah knew better. In the wintertime, in the evenings when there was little to do, Katherine read anything to do with medicine she could get her hands on. It was like a hobby with her.

"Brew Farley some tea," Katherine said to Moriah as they entered the bedroom together. "He looks like he could use some."

Camellia lay on the bed red-faced, panting and straining. Farley cowered beside her, his face pasty white.

"I don't like tea," Farley protested.

"Put plenty of sugar in it," Katherine instructed. "You've had a shock Mr. Kinker. Hot tea and sugar will help you get past it."

Moriah knew that Katherine didn't really care how Farley fared. Telling Moriah to fix him tea was her way of telling Moriah to get him out of the way. There was nothing that annoyed Katherine more than having someone hovering nearby in her way who couldn't be of any help. She especially didn't like having someone around who seemed likely to come down with the vapors—especially when it was a man.

One look at Farley, and Katherine wanted him out of the way.

"Come into the kitchen, Mr. Kinker." Moriah ushered the pale, shaking little man from the bedroom.

"I just don't understand it." He hung his head and stared at the floor while Moriah filled a kettle with water. "Camellia's never had any trouble before. All four boys came quickly. At home."

Moriah listened with half an ear as she searched the cabinets for a tea bag and a container of sugar.

More moans came from the bedroom as she and Farley waited for the water to came to a boil.

"Where did Camellia put the tea and sugar, Mr. Kinker? I remember she loved tea and always brought some with her."

"What?" He lifted his head.

"Tea? Sugar?"

"I think the boys ate all the sugar last night. I don't know where she put the stuff."

Heavy, guttural panting came from within the bedroom, followed by a thin, high-pitched squeal. Mr. Kinker's eyes grew large and the area around his mouth turned a sickly shade of green.

Moriah made a quick decision. "Go to the lodge, Mr. Kinker. There's tea and sugar in the canisters on the counter. Make some, drink it slowly, and then bring some back for your wife. She'll need it after the baby comes."

"Are you sure I should leave?"

"I'm sure."

The man nearly fell over his feet in his haste to leave the cabin.

After he left, Moriah glanced into the bedroom. Camellia's hair had come undone from its perpetual bun. It was now wet with sweat and stringing down her face and back. Her face was puffy

"Push harder, Camellia!" Katherine said, sharply.

Moriah's head jerked back in surprise. Her aunt never used that tone of voice.

"How's it going?" Moriah asked.

"Camellia's doing great," Katherine said, with strained cheerfulness.

From the sound of her aunt's voice, Moriah knew she was lying—for Camellia's sake.

"What can I do to help?"

Katherine motioned for Moriah to bend down where she could whisper into her ear.

"Go call an ambulance," Katherine whispered hoarsely. "We have to get her to a hospital."

"Don't move me!" Camilla had overheard. "It hurts!"

"Could I be of some help?" A clipped, male voice rang out from behind Moriah.

"Oh Nicolas! Thank God!" Katherine said. "It's a shoulder dystocia I think. A bad one."

Moriah moved out of the way while Nicolas pulled up the sleeves of his dress shirt and rushed into the small adjacent bathroom. Moriah stood back and heard water running.

"My antibiotic soap is on the sink, Nicolas."

"I've got it, Kathy."

Kathy? In spite of the crisis, Moriah was surprised. Katherine had never allowed anyone to call her that.

"Dr. Bennett will be in here in a moment, Camellia," Katherine said, soothingly. "He knows a great deal about difficult births. You're going to be fine, honey."

Camellia strained again, the awful keening sound filled the room.

"Help him get the gloves on, Moriah," Katherine barked. "There's a box in my basket. Camellia, push!"

Moriah glanced down as Camellia strained and the baby's head emerged. Then, strangely, it disappeared. Something wasn't right.

"Did you try the Woods Maneuver?" Nicolas accepted the gloves Moriah slipped on him and took Katherine's place at the foot of the bed. "Weren't you taught that in medical school?"

"I tried it twice but it wasn't successful," Katherine said.

The baby's head emerged once more and Nicolas slid his hand in beside it. Moriah heard Camellia scream and suddenly she could not bear to be in the same room a moment longer.

Moriah raced out of the door and to the lodge, where she placed a call for an ambulance. There were only two on the island and sometimes it took a while for one of them to get there. She hoped they would arrive in time.

Having never given birth or assisted at one, Moriah knew she was no expert in childbirth, but she did know that a shoulder dystocia was not good news. One of her friends had suffered through that kind of birth. It meant that the baby's shoulders were simply too big to crowd through the birth canal. It was rare but, without expert intervention, it could sometimes be fatal.

After running back to the Kinker's cabin, she heard Camellia continuing to cry out from behind the closed door, and Katherine and Nicolas's voices trying to encourage her.

There was nothing more she could do except wait, hope Nicolas knew what he was doing, and pray.

She sat down on the couch and bowed her head. Preacher Howard said it didn't work this way—that God didn't want to be brought out only for special occasions, but she couldn't help herself. It had always felt to her like God had enough to deal with, so she tended to try not to bother him except in emergencies. This situation definitely qualified as an emergency. The baby's life hinged on the next few seconds.

There are few sounds harder to bear than a mother's screams during a difficult birth...

...and few sounds are sweeter than a newborn baby's first cry.

Moriah's communication with God was interrupted by the wail of a gloriously indignant—but very much alive—newborn. Tears of relief stung her eyes.

In a few seconds, Katherine strode out with the infant wrapped in a clean towel and laid it in Moriah's arms.

"We have a little girl, Moriah. Hold her while Nicolas and I take care of Camellia."

"He called you Kathy," Moriah said. "He said you were in medical school."

"We'll talk later," Katherine said, and left the room.

The baby fussed and waved her tiny fists in the air. Coming into the world had been quite an ordeal. She needed a bath, a snack and her mommy.

"Soon, baby girl, soon," Moriah crooned. She stood up and paced the floor, bouncing the newborn gently in her arms. As she passed a window, she saw Farley strolling down the path with two teacups in his hand.

"I've decided I like tea now." Farley entered the cabin with both teacups in his hands.

"I don't think Camellia wants any quite yet," Moriah said. "Maybe in a few minutes."

He sat the extra cup on an end table. "I'm feeling a lot better. The trick is putting enough sugar in it. Oh," he eyed the baby, "it's here. Good. Maybe things can get back to normal again."

Then he calmly sat down and sipped his tea.

"Camellia had a really close call," Moriah said, annoyed with Farley's complacency. "If Dr. Bennett hadn't come when he did, you could have lost her."

"A doctor?" Farley seemed disturbed. "Where did a doctor come from?"

"That's not the point. You almost lost the baby and maybe Camellia. Dr. Bennett came along just in time to save their lives. You should be grateful."

"Camellia never had any problem having kids before," he muttered, taking another slurp of tea.

Katherine emerged from the bedroom, checked on the baby and saw Farley sitting on the couch.

"Dr. Bennett is finishing up," she told him. "Camellia needed quite a few stitches, but your baby is fine."

"And just how much is all this going to cost me?"

"I don't know." Exasperation laced Katherine's voice. "Why don't you come in and ask the doctor yourself."

"I think I'll just do that." Farley sat his teacup on a side table, got to his feet, hoisted his pants, and followed Katherine toward the bedroom where Dr. Bennett was administering stitches.

Moriah seriously enjoyed hearing the loud thud Farley made as he passed out cold before he even got through the bedroom door. Evidently he had encountered a sight that was a bit upsetting.

Katherine calmly stepped over him and went back to assisting Nicolas.

Moriah sat back down on the couch, cradling the newborn. She touched the baby's tiny button nose with her finger.

"Welcome to the big wide world, little girl." She smiled as the baby yawned, blinked and stretched.

Moriah leaned back against the couch, the baby tucked carefully into the crook of her arm, and replayed the past few minutes in her mind. She knew her aunt had a better than average knowledge of medical things, but she'd never once mentioned medical school. Why had Nicolas said that?

"How's it going?" Ben entered the cabin, bringing a rush of fresh air in with him. "I heard the yelling stop. I'm hoping that's a good sign?"

He saw Farley stretched out on the floor. "Oh."

Then he glimpsed the tiny bundle in Moriah's arms. "No wonder the yelling stopped. Is everyone okay in here?"

"Yes." Moriah sighed with relief. "Everyone's okay—except for Farley. He decided to check out for a while. Where are the boys?"

"Taking the Monopoly game back to the lodge. The game didn't turn out so well. Half of the pieces were missing. I promised to play Scrabble with them instead."

"I don't think we have Scrabble."

"You don't. I noticed that this morning." Ben grinned. "How long do you think it will take for the boys to figure it out?"

"Probably not long enough." Moriah pulled a corner of the towel away from the baby's tiny face. "Check this out."

Ben ignored Farley and sat down beside her to admire the baby.

"Boy or girl?"

"A little girl. She might be a football player someday. Her shoulders were almost too big to make it through the birth canal. Apparently, Dr. Bennett came just in the nick of time. I've never seen Katherine so scared. She didn't know what to do and that's unusual."

"Farley's a lucky man." Ben touched the infant's damp wisp of brown hair. "I'd love to have one of these someday."

"What? A little girl?"

"Girl or boy. It wouldn't matter. I'd just like to have a family of my own. I've lost both my dad and my uncle. It would be pretty wonderful to have a houseful of my very own kids someday."

Moriah looked into his eyes. He was dead serious.

"You're lonely," she said.

"Sometimes."

"But you've got a whole tribe depending on you back in the Amazon."

"I do. They treat me with respect. Sometimes I suspect they may even feel some love toward me, but they got along without me for a very long time and will continue to do so after I'm gone. They also have very tight-knit family groups and I'm not part of any of them."

There was a rustle near Ben's feet. They both looked down. Farley opened his eyes, saw them staring at him, and suddenly sat up. "What happened?" he said, rubbing his forehead.

"Your wife gave birth," Moriah said, calmly. "And you passed out."

"Congratulations, Farley," Ben said. "You have a beautiful, healthy little girl."

"A girl?" Farley let out a disgusted sigh as though he were greatly put-upon. "That means we'll have to buy girl clothes instead of using the boys' hand-me-downs."

"Perhaps instead of counting the cost, you should count your blessings," Ben said, softly. "Your wife and child are alive, mate. You should rejoice."

"I can't help it." Farley's voice was laced with self-pity. "I told Camellia not to get herself pregnant again, but she wouldn't listen."

Moriah was suddenly sorry she was holding the baby. It had been such a close call for Camellia. She had suffered much to bring this child into the world, and Farley was so ungrateful. She wished she could smack him.

She didn't have to. Ben was done dealing with the man. Apparently, Farley had managed to get on his last nerve. Ben stood up, reached down, grabbed a handful of Farley's shirt and lifted him easily with one hand until they were nose-to-nose and Farley's feet were no longer touching the ground.

"I said," Ben's voice was quiet but deadly. "Your baby girl is alive and so is your wife. Without Katherine and Dr. Bennett's help, you could be planning a funeral right now. Do you know how much funeral's cost, Farley?" He gave him a shake, still holding him in mid-air. "Do you? Let me tell you. A funeral costs a whole lot more than a few sweet little girl clothes."

Without warning, he dropped Farley, whose knees gave out from under him and he crashed back onto the floor.

Moriah's mouth hung open. She closed it and swallowed. Farley was not a big man, but he still had to weigh at least a hundred and forty pounds. Ben had held him up in the air like he weighed no more than a small sack of potatoes. If she didn't have the baby in her arms, she would have applauded.

Until this moment, she had no idea that her new friend had an angry bone in his body but, under the right circumstances, Ben was quite a force. Who knew?

"Daddy?" Four little boys tumbled into the room as Farley picked himself up off the floor for the second time.

"Way to go," Moriah whispered in Ben's ear as he sat back down beside her. He didn't acknowledge her comment. His breathing was rapid, and his jaw and fists were clenched. As angry as Ben appeared, she was impressed that the only thing he had done to Farley was give him a shake and a good talking to.

Farley tucked his wrinkled shirt into baggy pants, and regained a sliver of dignity as he pointed the boys toward Moriah. "Children, we have a new baby."

The boys rushed to Moriah's side to admire their latest sibling.

"Can we play with him?" the oldest one asked.

"Her," Moriah corrected. "You have a sister. And no, you can't play with her yet. She's still brand new."

They nodded soberly, accepting Moriah's judgement. Brand new things were rare in the Kinker household and not to be taken lightly.

Katherine stepped out of the bedroom, took one look at the children and quickly closed the door behind her.

"Your wife is stable, thanks to Dr. Bennett's skill. The baby is fine, as far as I can see. But they both need to go to the hospital for an evaluation. Camellia and your new daughter have been through quite an ordeal."

"But…"

"Farley," Ben warned. "Don't go there."

The bedroom door opened again and Nicolas strode past all of them. The children's eyes went wide as he ripped off bloody latex gloves, stepped on the pedal that opened the metal trashcan in the kitchen area, dropped them in, and let the lid drop with a bang.

"Excuse me, but Camellia wants to see her baby." Katherine lifted the infant from Moriah's arms and disappeared into the bedroom.

"Moriah," Dr. Bennett said, "Please go to the lodge and call an ambulance." He pulled a cell phone out of his pocket and waggled it with disgust. "Apparently there's no service here yet."

"I already did," Moriah said. "They should be here soon."

"Wait," Farley said, sidling away from Ben as though he feared being dangled in the air again. "Is it absolutely necessary to have an ambulance come?"

"Yes," Nicolas said, flatly. "Katherine and I will go with Camellia and the baby in the ambulance. I don't know how skilled the EMT team is on the island and I don't want to take any chances with her. Ben? You bring Moriah. The two of you can take Katherine home later. I'll stay at the hospital overnight just in case. Considering Mr. Kinker's propensity for fainting at inopportune times, it might be best if he stayed here with his children."

Moriah felt her chest tighten at Nicolas's instructions and her palms grew sweaty. The nearest fully equipped hospital was in Espanola. Across the bridge. On the mainland.

Not on Manitoulin Island.

"I'd rather not." Moriah said. "Farley can go. I'll stay here with the boys."

"You aren't still giving into that old problem are you, Moriah?" Nicolas sounded exasperated as he rolled down his shirt sleeves and buttoned the cuffs. "I expected you to outgrow that issue years ago."

"Nicolas." Katherine had just come back into the room. She placed a hand against his shoulder. "That's enough."

"What are you talking about?" Ben was puzzled.

"Moriah won't leave her safe place," Nicolas explained. "I doubt she's been off Manitoulin Island since she was five. Do I have that right, Moriah?"

"I can't see it's any of your business," Moriah said. She had stopped disliking Nicolas for a few moments while he saved the baby's life. Now her aversion came flooding back.

"How little you know." Nicolas's voice was edged with bitterness. "It was once very much my business."

The sound of a siren drifted into the cabin.

"Ben, you can drive Katherine's car," Nicolas hurriedly gave out assignments. "Farley, you can drive your own. Moriah... I guess you can stay here with the children."

A few minutes later, Moriah and the children watched the small caravan leave the resort. The ambulance was in front. Ben and Farley followed behind.

She felt humiliated as Ben drove past. It felt as though she were one of the children, watching the grownup drive away.

What was *wrong* with her? Why did she have to be this way?

The self-hatred she felt as she turned to deal with the Kinker boys was bitter and intense.

"What are you going to play with us?" the oldest boy demanded. "We couldn't find the Scrabble."

The last thing Moriah felt like doing right now was play with the Kinker boys.

"I have something in my room you might like to see," she said.

"You mean we get to go upstairs?"

They had never been allowed upstairs before.

"You'll have to be very good." She heard the ambulance turn on its siren as they pulled onto the main road. "But yes. You'll get to go upstairs."

"What is it you're going to show us?"

"The world." She hoped that spinning the huge globe and watching the countries slide slowly past would keep the boys entertained for a few minutes—perhaps long enough for her to compose herself and gather the strength to face spending the rest of the day with them. "I'm going to show you the world."

Chapter Twenty

. . . .

"Could you explain what Nicolas was talking about back at the resort—that thing about Moriah not leaving the island?" Ben shifted his body as he sat on the hard plastic hospital chair. He was finding it impossible to achieve a comfortable position.

The acrid smell of burnt coffee drifted across the room from an untended coffee pot, which made Ben's stomach churn. He wished he had remembered to bring his sunglasses. The headache he had acquired on the drive to the hospital was a killer.

Katherine sighed and dropped the magazine she had been staring at onto her lap. She had been clutching a tissue that she now began to nervously tear into small pieces.

"I guess you should know. To make a very long story short. Moriah was so traumatized by the death of both of her parents, she did not speak for two solid years," Katherine said. "She also refused to leave the island."

"Were you able to get her any kind of help?"

"I tried. At least I got her what little help there was that was available on the island back then. Moriah was so frightened by the loss of her parents, I tried to reassure her by telling her that, even though her parents were gone, she was safe. I told her that Manitoulin Island was the safest place in the world. I knew better, of course. There's nothing special about our island. Bad things can happen on Manitoulin Island just like anywhere else. But she was a child. I thought if I created a little bit of magic for her, it might help. Instead, I think I managed to make everything worse."

"She was only five when her parents died?"

Katherine nodded. "She had been talking in full sentences by the time she was three. Moriah was such an outgoing, happy little girl until we lost my brother and sister-in-law. I took her to our family doctor— we only had two here on the island at the time—and he said that, with enough reassurance and stability in her life, she would eventually outgrow the silence and fear."

"He was wrong?"

"Unfortunately, yes. A year later, when she still hadn't spoken, I heard there was a psychologist who had established a practice in Espanola. I tried to take her, but every time I started to drive over the bridge she would start screaming and couldn't seem to stop."

"That poor little girl." Ben's heart broke at the thought of Moriah being in such distress.

"She was never a spoiled child so I knew her terror was real. I always weakened and turned the car around. Maybe if I had hardened my heart and ignored her pain and gotten her to a real professional, she wouldn't have this problem now. I have so many regrets."

"But she must have begun to talk again sometime."

"Yes, eventually. The doctor was right about that, but she's never been able to make herself leave the island."

It was hard for Ben to accept the idea that such fear could reside in someone so competent, so outwardly stable, so physically strong.

"But Moriah is no longer a child."

"No, and she's built herself a good life on this island. Everyone respects and likes her. But she's dreadfully ashamed of this weakness. She refuses to speak to anyone about it. Not even to me anymore. It was cruel for Nicolas to bring it out into the open like that."

Ben was still trying to wrap his mind around the enormity of the problem. "She won't leave the island? For anything?"

"It's not a matter of *won't* leave the island, she *can't*," Katherine said. "There's a big difference. Every time she's attempted it—and as an adult she's attempted it many times— her body goes into a full-fledged panic attack that is so severe it has all the symptoms of a heart attack. I've watched her try so hard, but her body rebels each time."

Ben's temples ached badly from the drive and now this information was pounding in his brain as well.

"I've read a lot about it over the years," Katherine said. "I think that what Moriah is dealing with is a form of agoraphobia."

"That's when people can't leave their houses, right?" Ben said. "Moriah doesn't seem to have any problem doing that."

"She doesn't, thank goodness. But sometimes agoraphobia will present itself as the inability to leave a certain geographical location."

"Like the island," he said.

"Exactly. And sometimes other phobias get mixed in with it. Like a fear of bridges. That's a fairly common one for agoraphobics. Even footbridges can become an issue. The experts believe that this sort of thing is rooted in early childhood trauma."

"Seems like psychiatrists tend to believe that everything goes back to early childhood trauma, don't they?"

"Seems like it," Katherine said. "I haven't read anything about well-meaning aunts causing it—but I think I had a big part in making her the way she is."

"Sounds like you did the best you could," Ben said. "I'm sure Moriah was lucky to have you to care for her."

"I suppose so, but I think my father did her the most good. He was so patient, and he taught her many useful things."

"She's the most competent woman I've ever met," Ben said.

136

So, the woman who was taking over too many of his waking thoughts was incapable of leaving the island. It was hard to imagine, but he had no reason to think Katherine would make it up.

"You need to realize that if you do stay the summer to work on Nicolas's lighthouse project, when it is finished, if you go back to your other work, Moriah will stay here. Unless God grants us a miracle, she will always remain here."

As he digested the reality of all of this, Ben's head throbbed so badly he wished he could wrench it off his neck.

"How did her parents die again?" he asked dully.

Katherine hesitated and then avoided his eyes by staring down at the torn tissue which now lay scattered like snowflakes across her lap. "A plane crash."

Chapter Twenty-One

It was the sort of island day for which vacationers traveled hundreds and sometimes thousands of miles each summer. The lake made tiny kissing sounds as it gently lapped at the beach. The air was fresh and cool. Loons spoke to each other in their wild, reedy calls—a call echoed by Native American flute music playing on the CD player she'd placed inside the lighthouse. A sunrise was just peeping over the horizon. A pink sky, but so many different shades of pink reflected in the lake. Such a lovely view.

It would be even lovelier from the top of the light tower. The thought of climbing those steps yet again, in spite of the damage, was tempting.

The music floated out through the open window while she sat on the top step outside the light keeper's cottage. From here, she could see the resort clearly. No one was stirring yet.

That was a good thing. She didn't want to have to deal with anybody yet. Or—in the mood she was in right now—have to deal with anyone ever. She wished she could just live out here and have everyone leave her alone.

She could still feel the sting of Nicolas's harsh words as they sliced through her joy in the baby girl's birth. It had been humiliating.

There were so many different ways to be handicapped. So many different ways to be crippled. For some people, the disability was visible. It was hard to hide a wheelchair or crutches or a hospital bed. For some people, like her, the handicap was very carefully hidden away, but there it remained—a fear so paralyzing that no amount of rational thinking could dissolve it.

The problem with trying to keep her greatest shame hidden, was the energy it took to protect it. A secret such as she carried was a heavy load.

It was so much better to simply build and repair things instead of trying to deal with people. Nails that she pounded into wood stayed exactly where she put them. People did not. Nails didn't judge you. People did.

The morning sun, as it rose now on Lake Huron, distracted her with its soundless pageantry. The rays were turning from pink to gold, burnished with bright oranges and reds, magnified and reflected in the surface of the lake. The red was a little worrisome, there might be rain before the day was over, but still, it was an extravagant display that she never tired of watching. Being here, watching the sunrise from the steps of the cottage, had long ago become her greatest antidote to pain.

Her grandfather had taught her this.

"There's healing here," he said, the day after the doctors announced that he only had a few months left. "I've felt it ever since I was small. After I'm gone, if you start to feel sad, come here to this spot and remember what I said. And while you're at it, take time to remember how very much I love you."

She had been just shy of her thirteenth birthday, and life had felt very dark and unfair the day he broke the news to her.

"I don't think I can stand it, Grandpa," she'd said. "I can't bear to lose you."

"But it's only this old wrinkled body that's going away. It hasn't worked good for a long time. Kinda glad it's almost time to get me a new one," he chuckled. "When I see God, I'll ask him to make me good-looking this time."

"Don't talk like that, Grandpa," she said.

"Why not? It's just the way life is. My body will be gone, but my love for you will never go away. Just like my love for your grandmother and your parents have never gone away. Love is the only thing that matters, Moriah. Great love never goes away. It is eternal."

While R. Carlos Nakai's wilderness-sounding Canyon Trilogy flute music played softly inside the cottage, she began to feel her spirits lift, as the emotional cleansing she always felt here began to work its magic.

If her grandfather had lived, would she have gotten over her fear of leaving the island? If her parents had not been taken from her when she was so little, would she have grown up normal? How could losing one's parents create so much trauma that she would still be suffering the effects of it?

As she sat on the steps, remembering her grandfather's words about love, her mind drifted to Ben. He had occupied her thoughts an awful lot these past three days. The moment between them yesterday morning when they had admired the newborn baby together had been special. She had never been so attracted to a man before in her life, not like this. She felt as though she were being drawn to his very essence, to his soul and spirit.

Last night when he had confronted Farley for not valuing his good fortune in having a healthy baby and wife, she had seen another side to him. Ben was amiable, but he wasn't a pushover. Goodness! That moment alone, when he lifted Farley off the ground and gave him a good talking to was almost enough to make her fall in love with him.

The image of Ben with those four boys grouped around him yesterday morning as he told them stories was something she would remember for the rest of her life as well. He would make an excellent father someday, not to mention being a great husband to some lucky woman.

She was already three years older than her mother and father had been when they got married. Of course, they had grown up knowing each other. Ben and she had known each other for such a short time, but there had been a look in Ben's eyes each time they'd been together that made her think he was as interested in her as she was in him.

Then Nicolas had to go and make his big announcement about her weakness last night. Her cowardice. Her paralyzing fear. He had torn away the careful façade she had built over the years—the pretense that nothing was wrong with her. The truth of the matter was, there was a great deal wrong with her and now Ben knew about it.

He had been noticeably absent last night when he came home from the hospital.

He had gone straight to his cabin after they had all gotten back from the hospital. Katherine said it was because he had a headache, but Moriah suspected it was because he didn't want to be around her anymore. What man would? What man would want a woman who was so emotionally crippled that she could not bring herself to leave an island?

Silly. She reprimanded herself for taking up valuable time pondering Ben. It was ridiculous to even think about maybe falling in love with him. Ben was just a guest and would be leaving when the lighthouse project was finished. He would be going back to a place she would never see.

There were so many places she would never see.

It was a little chilly this morning and sitting on this stone step wasn't making her any warmer. She should go back to the resort and start in on a project—the lavatory in Cabin Six had a crack in it and needed to be replaced. Three kitchen tiles were coming loose in Cabin Three and needed to be re-glued. One of the poles where Katherine hung the sheets out to dry was leaning and needed to be reset.

There was plenty to do, but Nicolas had taken the heart right out of her last night.

"Want some company?" Ben, wearing jeans and a safari-like tan shirt, climbed up the porch steps, took off his sunglasses, dropped his scuffed leather backpack on the small porch and settled down close beside her.

"Where did you come from?" she asked. "I don't see a boat."

"I walked. Or at least I attempted to. After fighting my way through that tangle of trees and briars to get here, I can certainly understand why you prefer to take the boat." He pulled his backpack toward him and started undoing buckles.

"I figured you would want to sleep in after the big trip to the hospital."

"Nope." Ben pulled a grease-stained paper sack and a thermos out of the backpack. "Farley was clearing out the cabin and packing up the kids."

"Where was he taking them?"

"Camellia has a sister who lives up near Sudbury. The sister is a nurse and wants the family to come and recuperate at her house. Last night, Nicolas told Farley it would be okay to take Camellia and the baby there tomorrow. He says that if Camellia is doing well enough he thinks she can leave by then. The hospital agrees. The sister is coming to take the boys with her today. Farley will stay with Camellia until the hospital releases her."

"All of them? That poor sister!"

"I don't know. She came to the hospital last night and seemed capable of dealing with all seven of them, even Farley." He pulled something wrapped in a napkin out of the sack. "Fried egg sandwich. I thought you might be hungry."

"Thanks." Moriah took the sandwich with gratitude. She'd been too upset earlier this morning to eat, but now that Ben was here with her, and not treating her like a freak after learning about her problem, her appetite had come back.

"She's a stronger woman than I am if they are going to stay with her very long." Moriah took a big bite of the sandwich.

Ben poured a paper cup of cocoa and handed it to her. "I'm impressed you could get out of bed this morning after babysitting the Kinker boys most of yesterday."

"I didn't babysit them."

"Then who did?" Ben handed her a paper napkin before getting down to business with his own sandwich.

"I didn't babysit them, I hired them. You can get a lot of work out of those boys for a dollar."

With a fried egg sandwich in one hand, cocoa in the other, and Ben close beside her, Moriah watched the ever-changing lake and was surprised by realizing that she was feeling happy.

They ate in a silence broken only by the lapping of the lake and the raucous calls of dozens of seagulls wheeling above them.

"They want a handout," Moriah said. "But don't give it to them."

"You don't want me to feed them?" Ben tentatively held a morsel of food in the air. "That seems a little harsh."

"Better not." She pulled his hand down. "They'll call in all their relatives and overrun the place before you know it. They get annoyed with you when you run out of food. Seagulls are very rude."

He obligingly stuffed the rest of his sandwich into his mouth and then brushed off his hands and showed them, empty, to the seagulls. The birds, disappointed in not getting an easy meal, wheeled and squawked their disapproval above them, then went in search of a more promising food source.

"You know?" Ben said, after he'd swallowed the sandwich, stretched out his legs and leaned back on his elbows. "I always wanted to watch a sunrise with a beautiful woman. I didn't expect to have to fight my way through a half-mile of wilderness to get to her, but it was worth a few scratches and gouges to get here. Now, go ahead and tell me what you got the boys to do. I'm all ears."

There it was again. Ben had called her "beautiful". It always took her breath away when he used that word. It took her a moment to regain her bearings.

"Well," she had to think. "For starters, the two older ones got to rake our entire beach to prepare it for swimmers. I had the two younger ones go through all the games in the lodge's great room and make sure all the pieces were in the right boxes. For another dollar apiece, they vacuumed and dusted the entire lodge."

"Did they do a good job?"

"No—but I didn't tell them that. They were trying, and they really liked getting an entire dollar for each job accomplished."

"I should have thought of that. It would have been a whole lot easier than trying to play Monopoly with them while Camellia was trying to have her baby."

"How was Camellia and the baby last night?"

"When I left, everyone seemed to be doing well enough. They named the little girl 'Rosie' by the way."

'What about Katherine and Nicolas?'

"What about them?"

"How did they act?"

"You mean together? Katherine and Nicolas were a little self-conscious around each other at the hospital. Quiet. Professional. Nicolas kept looking like he wanted to say something, but never quite got the nerve. Katherine seemed determined to ignore him. It was all business between them. I thought the ice was broken once they had worked together to save little Rosie, but once Katherine had thanked Nicolas for his help, she grew cold toward him again, like she acted that first day when they met."

"I'm not wild about the man, of course," Moriah said. "I think I've made that pretty clear, but I've never seen Katherine act like this before. I wish I knew what was going on."

"Apparently they wish you didn't, or Katherine would have mentioned something about Nicolas a long time ago. She didn't say a word to me about him in the car coming home."

"Not a word?"

"Not about him. We talked a bit about the upcoming tourist season, but she was pretty much into her own thoughts. Should I have pried?"

"No," she said. "That would have been a mistake. I think it would be best to allow Katherine privacy for now."

It felt so good having him beside her. He was sitting close enough that she could smell the faint woodsy scent that usually clung to him. It wasn't overpowering, and she liked it very much.

"What's the name of that aftershave you wear?" she asked. "It's nice."

"I don't use aftershave."

"You must use something."

"What does it smell like?"

"I don't know. It's woodsy with some kind of spice."

"Oh," he said. "That's just my shaving soap. It has sandalwood in it. Taylor of Old Bond Street. It's what my dad and uncle always used, so I ended up using it too."

"The scent seems familiar to me, but I don't know why."

"Beats me. It would be unusual for you to come across it. Most men don't use a shaving brush and soap anymore, but I like it. When I was a little boy, it fascinated me to see my dad lather up. He'd hand the shaving brush to me to dab some on my face—and then, after he'd finished shaving and rinsed the razor off, he'd take the blade out and let me pretend to shave the soap off. It's a nice memory."

"So you use the same shaving soap that your dad did? That's sweet."

"No, it's practical. One of those bars lasts forever. With what I do, it makes a whole lot more sense than toting around a bunch of aerosol shaving foam cans." He laid his arm carelessly around her shoulder. "What are you doing out here today? Saying good-bye? Or avoiding me?"

"Why would I avoid you?"

"Possibly because of the look you gave Nicolas last night when he made an issue about you not being able to leave the island. He embarrassed you. I'm sorry he did that. Katherine explained it to me—about what happened after your parents died. I wish you hadn't had to experience that."

He kept his arm draped loosely around her shoulders. It was not a romantic gesture. It was simply the comforting touch of a friend. The warmth of his body felt exactly right against hers. It was only now that she realized how badly she'd wanted him to come and be with her this morning. How badly she'd needed him to let her know he was not repelled by her weakness, her cowardice, this weird form of agoraphobia that she struggled with.

She was too vulnerable when he was around. She was already starting to care too much about what he thought about her.

Chapter Twenty-Two

She had been so engrossed in her thoughts about Ben that at first she didn't notice the sky growing dark. When she saw that rainclouds were gathering, she thought of the old mariner's rhyme:

Red sky in morning, sailors take warning.

That rhyme had been drilled into her every time her grandfather stood at the resort window and looked out into a reddish early morning sunrise. Sometimes, if there was a reddish sky in the evening, he would quote:

Red sky at night, sailor's delight.

Then, they would talk about what all they would accomplish the next day because they knew the weather would be fine. The sunrise this morning had been especially spectacular, primarily because of all the reddish hues in it, but the sky had been so clear and blue she thought maybe the old rhyme was going to be wrong this time. Apparently it wasn't.

Even with storm clouds gathering overhead, she felt reluctant to leave the stalwart comfort of Ben sitting beside her here. Problem was, that sky wasn't going to hold off for long.

"Are you going to give me a ride in that boat, lass, or make me walk back through all that overgrowth?" Ben's voice broke into her thoughts.

It was the sky that decided her next actions as small droplets of rain began to hit them.

"Let's get inside." She jumped up. "The roof on the old office is still intact. At least enough, I think, to keep us out of the rain. It wouldn't be wise to head out onto the lake right now. Too much danger of lightning. You don't want to be sitting in a metal boat when lightning starts to strike."

"No, I don't." Ben quickly gathered up the napkins and sack, crumpled them and stuffed the wad of paper into his pants pocket. Then he grabbed the empty thermos. "That's an adventure I would rather avoid."

At the clap of thunder, they scrambled into the cottage and Moriah led him through the ruined, empty rooms to the old, lighthouse office. Unlike the rest of the dwelling, the one window in the office room had been left whole and only a tiny rivulet of water ran down the stone wall. The only thing in the room except themselves was the fireplace and hearth, and a large wooden desk built into a corner.

Ben and Moriah stood in the middle of the room and listened to the thunder volley off the stones of the cottage.

"That's pretty intense," Ben said.

"It gets that way out here." Moriah grabbed hold of Ben's arm as a sudden flash of lightning struck close by. She quickly released it and apologized. "Sorry."

"You didn't hurt me, lass," Ben chuckled. "That strike about made me jump out of my skin too. Did you, by any chance, happen to check what the weather was going to be today? Any tornadoes predicted? Hurricanes? Earthquakes?"

"It never occurred to me. I felt the need to be here, so I came."

"I think we might be stuck here for a while," he said. "I hope you don't mind, because I certainly don't."

"Is standing around in a damp, cold, lighthouse while it pours buckets of rain outside your idea of a good time?"

"No, but it's a lot better than sitting outside of a damp, cold, lighthouse while it pours buckets down your neck. Besides, I have you for company. That's always a bonus."

"I'll show you a family secret if you won't tell."

"Your family has secrets?" Ben said. "I would never have guessed."

Moriah punched him lightly on the shoulder. "Don't judge."

Then she turned around and wriggled a small stone out of the face of the fireplace directly behind her.

Ben folded his arms as he watched her. "This should be interesting."

"It will be." Moriah reached inside of the hole created by the removal of the stone and brought out an old iron key.

Ben watched with interest. "Does the key open a pirate's chest? Is there a treasure map? Perhaps a hidden staircase in here?"

"Sorry." She polished the key on her jeans. "No treasure map. No pirate's chest. No hidden staircase."

"What then?"

"The key opens a compartment in the bottom of that desk in the corner. The desk was built into the wall and was too cumbersome to move out when the lighthouse was shut down. In the end, Grandpa simply locked it up and put the key back where he always kept it—behind the loose stone. Of course, he showed me where it was."

"I'm surprised someone didn't take a crowbar to it to get into it."

"I don't think anyone else knew the compartment was there. My great-great grandfather, Liam Robertson, built the desk. From what I understand, he had been a ship's carpenter once. Apparently, a good one. He lined the compartment with cedar and my family kept things in there they thought valuable."

Moriah knelt in front of the desk and fit the key into an invisible lock that was hidden well beneath the desk. There was a small click as she turned the key.

"I've never seen a desk designed like that." Ben ran his hand over the scarred surface.

"Grandpa said you could tell that the man who built it had spent time on a ship because of the sturdy way it is designed. Underneath all the dirt, it is made out of seasoned red oak and is as hard as a rock."

A door swung open beneath the desk and Ben caught a faint whiff of cedar. Moriah reached deep inside and pulled out a thick sleeping bag, a folded blanket and a pillow. She arranged it all in front of the fireplace and sat down cross-legged on it.

"I'll share." She patted the seat beside her.

Ben happily settled in next to her. He looked at the fireplace where a stack of logs and kindling lay.

"I wish we had some matches."

"Do you want a fire?" she asked.

"It would be nice. Especially if it continues to rain."

"You underestimate me, McCain." Moriah rose and dug into the deep recesses of the desk again, producing a clean mayonnaise jar filled with small boxes of safety matches. She held out her hand. "Give me that sack you stuffed in your pocket right before we came inside, please."

Using the grease-stained paper wrappers from their meal beneath the dry kindling and logs already stacked in the fireplace, Moriah created a blaze in minutes.

"You were the one who stacked those logs here?" Ben said.

"You never know when you'll need a good fire," Moriah said. "Sometimes in the summer our guests start getting on my last nerve and I come out here for a while. I always keep a few supplies here so I'll be able to have a getaway."

Everything felt better and more cheerful as they sat near the fire watching it blaze against the storm. Eventually, the fire grew so hot that they moved farther away from the hearth, propping themselves against the opposite wall with the sleeping bag beneath. They watched the fire burn, sometimes popping and cracking almost in unison with the lightning. The rain thrummed steadily on the slate roof.

"How long have you been keeping things like this out here, Moriah?"

"From the day Aunt Katherine allowed me to come out here by myself."

"You were…"

"Thirteen and miserable. That was the year my grandpa died. It didn't happen all of a sudden. Katherine and I took care of him for several months. Sometimes watching him go downhill would get to be too much and I'd have to escape out here until I could pull myself together. Then I'd go back and help."

"Who cared for the resort then? You?"

"Not entirely. I was still a kid." She yawned. "We hired a man."

"Sleepy?"

"A little. I had a hard time getting to sleep last night."

The wind audibly changed directions and rain pelted against the window. Thunder hovered and grumbled directly above them.

Ben scooted to the far end of the sleeping bag, took the pillow and laid it down beside him.

"Lie down."

"What?"

"Lie down and sleep. I'll watch over you and your lighthouse while you take a nap."

"You sure?"

"I'm sure."

Moriah didn't fight it. The crackling of the fireplace and the roll of thunder had created a sort of lullaby to her. She laid her head on the pillow and pulled the blanket over her shoulders. The rain sounded like it had settled in to stay. There was no way they could leave until it stopped.

But when she closed her eyes, she found that she couldn't drift off after all. She was too aware of Ben's nearness.

"Tell me about where you live."

He began to gently stroke her hair. She didn't mind.

"What do you want to know?"

"Everything. Every detail. I want to know what the people wear, what the trees look like, what they eat. What it sounds like and smells like. Everything."

"I don't know if I can tell you everything." There was a smile in his voice. "Even if it rains a really long time."

"Then tell me something. Apparently I'll never see anything except Manitoulin Island. I'd like to hear details about some faraway place—especially the one where you live."

"Well, okay, then." He paused. "It is more beautiful than you can imagine, Moriah, and more dangerous than most people ever realize."

Listening to Ben's voice while she lay gazing into the fire felt delicious. Even though they were caught in a tumbledown cottage with torrents of rain sluicing all around them... she didn't remember ever feeling so warm and safe.

"How is it dangerous?" She pushed the blanket down to her waist. It was beginning to grow warm in the small office.

"In so many ways. For instance, have you ever heard the old saying that both fish and guests start to stink in three days?"

"Aunt Katherine has said that a few times about certain guests."

"I bet she has." Ben chuckled. "Sometimes it's true even with primitive tribes. If they are at peace at the time, they're happy to see a foreigner the first day you arrive. You are new and interesting. The second day, you're still fairly welcome. By the third day the novelty has worn off and they've grown tired of entertaining you. Especially if they are responsible for feeding you. Most of the tribes live a subsistence lifestyle at best and even a handful of outsiders can quickly deplete their food stores. If a traveler doesn't take the hint and move on, he or she can find themselves in mortal danger."

"Still? In this day and age?"

"Still," Ben said. "I have felt threatened more than once when I've traveled outside my tribe's geographical area, even when I didn't overstay."

"Why does the Yahnowa allow you to live with them?"

"I bring my own provisions, of course. They don't have to feed me. But primarily they allow me to stay because of the great work a young medical missionary did. She's the one who first began to live among the Yahnowa. They loved her. It opened up opportunities for others to minister to them, including me."

"And Nicolas. It's hard to imagine him in that situation."

"Nicolas may not be easy to talk to, and I agree that he can be a little arrogant—but he's trying to do some good things. I got the impression he had received a rather large inheritance from his wife and, along with his own savings, he's looking for positive ways to use it."

Moriah didn't want to hear any more about Nicolas. She wanted to hear about Ben. His life. His work. "So you're completely alone there?"

"I'm never alone. There's always and forever, God, who has become especially real to me these past five years. Plus there are the Yahnowa people, whom I love and respect. Then, there's Abraham Smith, a retired minister, and his wife, Violet. They are an older couple that settled there about eight years ago. They use their retirement income to support themselves. He tries to teach the Yahnowa and she was a nurse most of her life. She does what she can with some basic medical supplies."

"I wish I could see it someday."

Ben's hand, which had been stroking her hair, stilled. "I wish you could, too."

He began describing the flowers and trees, animals and people in his village. His voice soothed her, a lullaby of words, and she drifted off.

* * *

When he saw that she was sound asleep, Ben stopped talking. He had not gotten much sleep either. All he could think about was the revelation he had received from Nicolas and Katherine. There was a good chance, a very good chance, that Moriah would never be strong enough emotionally to leave the island. Falling in love with her could get a bit awkward.

Who was he kidding? Falling in love with Moriah would be devastating. Life would be much simpler if he wasn't so fascinated with her.

The position in which he was sitting began to feel uncomfortable. He stood and walked over to the small window and looked outside. It was too dark to see anything, until a bolt of lightning streaked through the air and for one quick moment lit up an image of the lake lashing against the shore.

How many people had stood here in this spot, looking out at the wild fury he was witnessing? How many times had the various light keepers had to leave the solid sanctuary of the stone lighthouse to man a rescue boat when a ship went down. Had Eliza, Moriah's ancestor, ever done such a thing in those early years when she cared for the lighthouse?

He could see Moriah risking her life in a rowboat to save others. He was fairly certain she wouldn't hesitate or consider her own peril. To think that this strong, young woman couldn't manage to leave her island refuge was ridiculous—except for the fact that it was true.

He turned from the window and watched the firelight play over her face. He was grateful that she was getting some rest. The past couple of days had been hard on her. Sleep might make it easier for her to deal with things.

There was a sketchpad in his backpack. He had brought it to make rough drawings of the various changes Moriah had considered making to the place. Before he began the work, he wanted to make sure

Nicolas approved her ideas. For instance, she'd mentioned turning the foghorn room into a combination study and bath. That would need to be drawn out and discussed. It was the main reason he'd come out here this morning.

Now, sitting across from her, watching the shadows and light from the fire dancing over her face and body, he was caught up in the desire to draw her—just as she was—hair all tangled from the boat ride across the lake, eyes closed. Completely unaware that he was studying her.

Ben had never considered himself an artist, but he had developed an ability with pen and pencil over the years that came in handy when he was trying to envision a project, or capture an idea of a client. This was easier for him to do than most because, from the time he was a child, he had entertained himself by drawing whenever there was a lull in school, or whenever he was alone and needing to entertain himself.

Now, he wished he'd actually taken real art classes so he could capture this image of Moriah exactly as she was right now.

Oh well. It was just for him. It didn't have to be perfect. He didn't even need to ever show it to anyone. He placed another log on the fire and punched up the glowing embers so he would have more light. Then, as the rain continued to beat against the roof, he settled back against the wall with his sketchpad on his knees and began to sketch.

* * *

Moriah and her best friend, Karyona, lay together in the sleeping hammock, their little girl arms and legs entwined. Light from the fire that Karyona's parents kept in the middle of the hut danced on the ceiling. Moriah was having a great deal of trouble getting to sleep. It was hard to even close her eyes when she was so excited.

Today was her fifth birthday and, since she was such a big girl now,

Mommy had allowed her to sleep over in Karyona's hut. It was the first time, ever, that she'd slept apart from Mommy and Daddy. Being here by herself felt a little strange, but she was determined to make it through the night without asking to go back to them. She was a big girl now, and needed to be brave. Besides, this was something she had been begging to do for weeks.

"Do you think there's any reason not to let her?" Mommy had asked Daddy.

"Not that I can see," Daddy said. "We are close by. If she gets frightened it will only take Akawe a moment to bring her to us."

Akawe was Karyona's daddy, and Napognuma was her mommy. Their hut was directly across from the clinic Mommy and Daddy were helping Doctor Janet build. They were Christians and Napognuma helped Mommy sometimes. There was much to learn about living in the Amazon forest, and Napognuma knew everything there was to know. Mommy loved learning about all the plants and animals. She said it was all so different from Manitoulin Island.

"If you get scared, have Akawe bring you back," Mommy said, smiling and giving her a hug as she left her at Karyona's hut. "Sometimes little girls change their minds on their first sleepover and need to come home. If that happens, it's all right, no one will mind."

Moriah played with some of Karyona's hair as she lay there curling it around and around her finger, listening to the even breathing of all of Karyona's family. They all lived together in one room. Her big brother, Rashawe, slept there, too. Rashawe was old. Already fifteen and a very good hunter.

Moriah wished her mommy and daddy and Doctor Janet and Petras could all sleep in the same room like Karyona's family. She had suggested it at dinner, but her mommy shushed her and said that big people needed to sleep in separate rooms. Moriah didn't see why. It was nice having *everyone all together.*

Moriah wriggled her toes with pleasure. She loved living here with the Yahnowa people in the winter. She especially liked getting to play all day outside with the other children instead of being cooped up in the lodge back home.

She had a pet monkey here, too!

Last winter the fluffy snow at home was taller than her head and she had to stay inside the lodge all day every day for weeks and weeks. She hated not getting to go outside.

But this winter was different. Daddy had packed his best carpentry tools. Then they came in a big airplane to the jungle to help build another room on Doctor Janet's clinic.

Doctor Janet was pretty but Moriah didn't think she was as pretty as Mommy. Mommy had big blue eyes and curly black hair and very light skin. Daddy teased Mommy and called her a paleface because he was part Ojibwa and had shiny black straight hair and skin that was brown and never burned. Just like Moriah's. Mommy always teased her and said that she was terribly jealous of Moriah's beautiful skin and good looks that she had inherited from her daddy.

She liked taking after her daddy. It made her feel special when they were together and people looked at them and laughed.

"Spitting image," they would say.

She had no idea what spitting had to do with looking like her daddy, but she liked how proud he acted when people said that.

The Yahnowa called her "Little Green Eyes" because her eyes were the only thing that set her apart from the other black-haired, brown-skinned children in the village. She liked having a special name.

It was fun here. She was able to blend in with the other children so well that her mother allowed her to dress like them, which meant wearing very little. Her daddy had frowned, but her mother had said, "Oh goodness, Jake, she's only five—let her be. She'll grow up soon enough. Let her be a wild child for these few weeks."

That's how she liked to think of herself as she played with the other village children. She was a wild child.

She took the strand of Karyona's hair between her fingers and twisted it together with a strand of her own. They were both puddles of black in the moonlight. All around Moriah were the sounds of Karyona's family sleeping. She wondered why Mommy said big people had to have separate rooms.

She was just dozing off when she heard a sharp crack outside of the window and a quick shuffling sound. Wild animals sometimes snuffled around the village at night but this sounded different. She lifted her head, straining to hear.

The muffled sounds moved away. Then a light flickered against the wall of the hut through the cracks between the bamboo poles of the wall. Moriah heard a shout, then another one and then a scream. The scream sounded exactly like Mommy the day she'd found a snake under her bed.

Moriah struggled to sit upright in the hammock. Had Mommy found another snake? In the middle of the night? Daddy would kill it like he'd killed the last one and would tease Mommy about her reaction to it in the morning.

Then shouts filtered through the bamboo wall and made her feel really, really scared. Maybe there were a lot of snakes over at the clinic. She thought she heard her father yelling now.

Silently, she slipped out of Karyona's hammock and padded to the door. Moriah opened it just enough to see out. She knew she wasn't supposed to go outside after night, and she wouldn't, but she didn't think she would get in trouble by just looking.

What she saw through the slit in the door had nothing to do with snakes and everything to do with men lifting machetes up and down while Daddy and Petras tried to protect Mommy and Janet. But Daddy and Petras didn't have machetes, they just had hands and their hands and faces were bloody. The bad men kept bringing the machete down over and over and Mommy was crawling and Daddy was trying to go to her and...

She couldn't see her mommy and daddy anymore. Petras had backed against the door that Moriah had been looking through. He was grunting and fighting the bad men with his big fists. She wanted Petras to fight hard. Petras was big. Bigger and stronger than Daddy. Maybe he could win against the bad men. Moriah knew they were bad men now, bad Yahnowa men with painted faces.

Hot urine ran down her leg, soaking into the dirt floor.

"Petras!" she screamed, but a hand went over her mouth and shut off the scream. She felt herself lifted away from the door and carried to the far side of the hut to the platform where Karyona's mommy and daddy slept. She tried to get away, but Akawe held her tightly, with his hand firmly over her mouth.

Tears came then, tears of anger and fear. They dribbled over Akawe's hand and ran down onto Moriah's neck while he kept her immobilized and silent. Napognuma had pulled Karyona out of her hammock and now held her in her arms, rocking back and forth, staring at the closed door. Fifteen-year-old Rashawe, already a warrior, crouched in front of the door, a spear in his hand.

"Chief Moawa," Karyona's daddy whispered to Napognuma as Moriah struggled and kicked to get away. "He must not find out that we shelter the white child."

* * *

"No!" Moriah screamed, desperately fighting the hands that

restrained her, kicking at the blanket tangled around her feet. "Mommy!"

"Shush, Moriah, sweetheart, you're just having a bad dream."

Disoriented, Moriah sat up and gazed around wildly. The room felt alien to her. There was a wood floor instead of packed dirt. Stone walls instead of bamboo. She didn't know where she was. She wasn't entirely certain *who* she was.

"Petras?" she said to the big, solid, red-haired man beside her.

"That was my father's name, honey. I'm Ben."

She realized that she was drenched in sweat. "Where am I?"

"You're in the lighthouse cottage. There's been a thunderstorm, and you've been having the worst nightmare I've ever seen. I couldn't wake you for the longest time."

Moriah drew Ben's hands into her own and examined them. "You have Petras's hands." She touched a strand of his hair that had fallen over his forehead. "You have Petras's hair."

"Why are you talking about Petras?" Ben said. "Who is he to you?"

"He was fighting." Moriah's brain was still fuzzy from the nightmare. She fought to come fully awake but the nightmare was still so fresh upon her that she felt as though she were still partially in it. "He was fighting for his life... and my mother's... and Doctor Janet's... and I think... at the very last... he was fighting for me. I know it had to be a nightmare, but it felt real. So very real."

One last volley of thunder hit, along with a streak of lightning that lit up the room and Moriah began to tremble.

Ben gathered her up in his arms and held her against him. Rocking her. Comforting her.

"Do you know what my father's name was, Moriah?" Ben asked, softly. "Have I ever mentioned it to you?"

"No," she answered against his chest. "You've talked about your dad, but you never said his name."

"My father's name was Petras," Ben said, tears choking his voice. "And I know absolutely that he would have fought for you."

Author's Note

I was surprised to discover that during the 1800's and early 1900's, an era when it was taken for granted that a woman should be paid less than a man, over a hundred women kept the lights burning in lighthouses all over the United States and Canada. Most were women who were already familiar with the job, and who were granted the right to continue the work of their deceased husbands and fathers. They were given pay equal to their male counterparts long before women won the right to vote.

Many took on this hazardous job while also raising large families. Most impressive of all were the women who rowed out alone in storms to rescue those who would otherwise have perished.

Sometimes they faced starvation in the north when the ships that tended the lights could not break through the spring ice to bring provisions. They made hundreds of weary trips up staircases to carry fuel and supplies to keep the light burning. They went without sleep night after night to ensure the lights did not go out. They struggled with loneliness, danger, sickness, sleeplessness, and isolation while keeping those beacons of hope and guidance shining out upon the turbulent waters.

It is impossible to calculate the vast numbers of lives and ships they saved.

Modern day people love the romantic notions of lighthouses. The endurance and dedication of the old light keepers grabs the heart and excites the imagination. Many history buffs devote much of their lives to researching and preserving the lore and history of our remaining lighthouses.

As I researched this series of books, that fact created a problem for me as an author. I try to record the settings of my books as accurately as possible. In this case, it was my beloved Manitoulin Island that I wanted to describe. I did not think choosing an existing lighthouse as a backdrop for a fictional family was going to be well-received by those who have meticulously researched the struggles of the actual families who lived in specific lighthouses.

So, I made one up.

I chose the general location of Providence Bay (which I rename Tempest Bay) where a lighthouse once stood before it burned down. I took great license with the immediate area, creating a peninsula and nearby fishing resort that does not exist. The characters I put in the lighthouse were not based on anyone I know. Michael's Bay (which I rename Gabriel's Bay) is Manitoulin's only ghost town.

Lighthouses similar to the one I describe do exist, however. I chose to pattern Moriah's lighthouse after the Imperial Towers built around the Great Lakes in the early 1800's. They had the stonework that I needed for the story. I read extensively and visited Great Lakes lighthouses to be as accurate as possible in my descriptions. I apologize to lighthouse historians for any mistakes I might have made.

The Yahnowa tribe where Ben lives and works does not exist. However, I tried to make the customs, habits, and habitats as believable and accurate as possible based on my research into some of the larger Amazonian rainforest tribes. A warning, though. Studying the treatment of the indigenous tribes of the Amazon is heartbreaking.

The phobia with which Moriah struggles, does exist. My hope is that as we watch her battle against fear unfold, it might help us face our own demons with a bit more courage.

–Serena

My Heartfelt Thanks To:

Charlie Robertson, owner of the once-famous rock shop on Manitoulin Island. I appreciate the example you have been of choosing joy in spite of great loss.

Mamie (Coriell) Robertson, my transplanted cousin, who followed her heart to Manitoulin Island to be with Charlie. Thank you for telling us about the island so many years ago.

Wanda Whittington, Charlie's granddaughter. Thank you for patiently sharing your knowledge of your beloved Manitoulin Island with me and for your amazing hospitality.

My family, for taking the time to help me explore and research the island. The depth of your continued support and encouragement continues to astonish and humble me.

My church who so lovingly took care of me and my family during my husband's final illness.

About the Author

Best Selling author, Serena B. Miller, has won numerous awards, including the RITA and the CAROL. A movie, Love Finds You in Sugarcreek, was based on the first of her Love's Journey in Sugarcreek series, and won the coveted Templeton Epiphany award. Another movie based on her novel, An Uncommon Grace, recently aired on the Hallmark channel. She lives in southern Ohio in a house that her husband and three sons built. It has a wraparound porch where she writes most of her books. Her mixed-breed rescue dog, Bonnie, keeps her company while chasing deer out of the yard whenever the mood strikes. Her Manitoulin Island series is a labor of love based on many visits to the beautiful island.

www.serenabmiller.com

More books by
Serena B. Miller

LOVE'S JOURNEY ON MANITOULIN ISLAND SERIES:

Love's Journey on Manitoulin Island: Moriah's Lighthouse - Book I
Love's Journey on Manitoulin Island: Moriah's Fortress - Book II
Love's Journey on Manitoulin Island: Moriah's Stronghold - Book III

LOVE'S JOURNEY IN SUGARCREEK SERIES:

Love's Journey in Sugarcreek: The Sugar Haus Inn - Book I
   (Formerly : Love Finds You in Sugarcreek, Ohio)
Love's Journey in Sugarcreek: Rachel's Rescue - Book II
Love's Journey in Sugarcreek: Love Rekindled - Book III

THE UNCOMMON GRACE SERIES (*AMISH*):

An Uncommon Grace - Book I
Hidden Mercies - Book II
Fearless Hope - Book III

MICHIGAN NORTHWOODS SERIES (*HISTORICAL*):

The Measure of Katie Calloway - Book I
Under a Blackberry Moon - Book II
A Promise to Love - Book III

SUSPENSE:

A Way of Escape

COZY MYSTERY:

The Accidental Adventures of Doreen Sizemore

NON-FICTION:

More Than Happy: The Wisdom of Amish Parenting

VISIT **SERENABMILLER.COM** TO SIGN UP FOR
SERENA'S NEWSLETTER AND TO CONNECT WITH SERENA.

4 g

CPSIA information can be obtained
at www.ICGtesting.com
Printed in the USA
LVOW12s2303040917
547547LV00001B/32/P